Other books by Serg Koren:

Last Call
The Roland Targus Series
The Treasure
The Curse
The Kingdom
The Couple
Puffin and Griswold in the Tunnel of Darkness.

SCAVENGER HUNT

SERG KOREN

Published by BookBaby

Print ISBN: 978-1-66785-178-5
eBook ISBN: 978-1-66785-179-2

Printed in the United States of America

First Edition

To friends and family. You know who you are.

TABLE OF CONTENTS

CHAPTER 1 - LANCE GARNER

"SH-1 to SH-2." Lance Garner brings the rifle up to firing position, scoping the pile of slag and rock that had been a building a hundred years or more ago. The bud in his ear that acted as both a microphone and speaker crackles and the gravel-like voice of his second in command responds, tinny but audible.

"SH-2 to SH-1. I have movement incoming. Half-click." Kingston Sharman's large voice matched his personality and form. "Ugly-looking sucker."

Lance, SH-1, catches something loping at the edge of the mound. "SH-2, I have visual. I don't have a shot. How about you?" The target moves fast and shifts direction as it runs.

"Negative, Viper. I won't until it clears the debris. What's it doing?"

Viper is Lance's call sign. Lance adjusts the sight on the rifle. "Hard to tell. It's just moving back and forth."

"There's nothing in that mess worth having, is there?"

"Can't think of anything a scavenger would want." Lance keeps the scope on the target, hoping for a clear shot. The brim of his cap shades his eyes and neck from the sun's radiation. If the levels were high, the brim would have shifted color and snapped down. The creature stops moving, and Lance sees it is staring down at the ground. He has his shot. He lines up the crosshairs and flips the safety.

"SH-1 to SH-3. You have a group of nasties moving fast toward our location."

"Shit." Lance curses as he resets the scope's zoom to its lowest setting. "How many, Oversight?"

"I count maybe twenty—wait—twenty-five a click away. You need to get out of there." Oversight, whose name is Deforest Morison and who is the team member responsible for protecting their backs, is the youngest one. Despite Deforest's age, Lance has trusted him with his life on more than one occasion. "They'll be on us in a minute or two."

"SH-1 to SH-2. Boomslang, you copy? We need to abort."

"Viper, we can take them. We've done more." Deforest is always itching for a fight, be it a simple brawl or a firefight.

"Viper, if we are going to move, we need to do it now. Nasties are closing fast."

"How did they figure out we were here?" Boomslang's voice crackles over the bud.

"Worry about that later. I'm scrubbing the party. Head for the wheels." Lance shoulders his rifle and sprints for the two-track they had hidden in a clump of scraggly orange-colored trees. He curses again. This was supposed to be an easy hunt: take out one lone scavenger but make sure the brain remained intact. Gov wanted it badly enough that he had put a bounty out to every hunter who wanted to try. Their team had lucked out when their scanner had spotted the heat signature of the lone scavenger. They traveled in packs and the easiest way to kill them was a bullet through the brain. Lance is in shape, but the kilometer-long sprint to their vehicle still had made him puff. The constant heat and humidity has taken a toll on everyone regardless of their physical health.

Lance catches sight of the other two team members converging on the same spot. It would have been nice to have tagged the target, but their safety overrode any desire for the bounty. That's why the team had survived as long as it had, longer than most. They didn't take unneeded chances. They might not like playing it safe, but they enjoyed being alive more. Too many others had underestimated the scavengers, or gotten too greedy trying for a kill, only to be overwhelmed by the fast-moving enemy.

Oversight's voice breaks into Lance's thoughts. "Big trouble, Boss. We have another group converging on us. Can't tell yet how many. We need to blow."

"You heard the man, Boomslang. Time to call it a day." Boomslang, to his right, clicks his bud on and off to indicate he heard, but that also means he isn't happy about it.

The three reach the armored vehicle within a second or two of each other. Oversight's hat brim is down, as it is most of the time on a mission. The built-in HUDs provide the intel and readouts they need. Lance can't see his expression through the dark glass, but he hears hesitation in his voice. "I think we have bigger problems."

Lance's attention snaps to the young man. "What now?"

The response has a few seconds' delay as Oversight rechecks his instruments. "Rad wave incoming. Biggest mother I've ever seen. I had to look twice to make sure my gear was okay."

"How bad?"

"Force 7. The wheels won't help us. We need to find deep shelter."

"Shit." Viper keys the access code into the vehicle's door panel. "All right, boys and girls, time to get in the bug and get out of here unless you want to get the sunburn of your life. Oversight?"

"I'm on it, Boss, checking the data banks for a safe spot." The three men clamber into the vehicle that looks like a cross between a turtle and snowplow. Lance flips switches and powers the vehicle's engines and weapons to life.

CHAPTER 2 - LANCE

Boomslang climbs into the back, where he mans the enclosed gun portal. Oversight's faceplate flips up to reveal a sandy-haired man with gray eyes as his suit's systems transfer control to the panel in the bug. "No official shelters in the area. There is an underground cavity about a day away at full speed to the northwest of our position. Feeding you the coordinates."

"What is it?" Lance asks.

"Intel isn't sure what it is, just that it was a complex of some sort."

"What about the nasties?" Viper asks as he engages the bug's two tracks.

"30 seconds. Boom, you ready?" Deforest calls over his shoulder to the large, burly man behind the gun's controls.

"Send 'em to me and I'll send 'em to hell."

"Just keep your head down," Viper commands as he guns the engine of the bug. The vehicle lurches before springing forward out of the trees onto bare ground. What roads there are are packed dirt. The war had done more than destroy the buildings. It had erased all signs of civilization in the country. It wasn't postapocalyptic since the rest of the world had survived fine outside the war.

"Nasties at one o'clock," Oversight barks. For added emphasis, he indicates the correct direction with a hand. He isn't sure what directions have to do with time, but he learned the system at a young age and is comfortable with it.

Viper grunts a thanks as he spots the creatures loping toward them. He points the nose of the bug at them and guns the engine. Even being run over wouldn't kill them unless the bug hit the head. The vehicle races forward, as does Lance's heart rate. He'd been in his early twenties, about Oversight's age, when he went out on his first hunt. He'd killed many of the creatures, more than most, but somehow it never had the thrill it had the first time. Now it was just part of his job, which was keeping the team alive. Boomslang's turret roars to life as the distance closes between the bug and the scavengers. Kingston is smart enough not to waste ammo.

The ground is rough and the bug bounces into the air and hits the ground hard, rattling those inside. Viper sees two of the creatures' heads rip open and splatter as Boomslang's bullets bite them. The scavengers don't realize they are already dead and continue to run for several yards before collapsing. Those behind them ignore their fallen comrades and continue to rush after the bug.

"What happened to the other group?" Viper snaps at Oversight.

"Falling behind. We just have to get through this bunch, then we have a clear shot to the underground."

Lance nods but says nothing. He focuses his attention on the long-legged, long-armed creatures in front of him. He sees a couple falter but continue forward. Missed head shots ring out from Boomslang. He's usually better than this. The distance between the scavengers and the bug closes at an increasing pace. "Hold tight. We're going through." Viper's team has done this before, but that didn't mean it was easy. The natural armor of the scavengers could take pretty much anything short of a thermal grenade—and those didn't come cheap. The creatures had evolved or mutated, Lance isn't sure which—he isn't a whitecoat—to the point it had become lightweight and dense. That made the scavengers hard to kill.

The lead creature hits the plow-shaped portion of the bug and flies up onto the armored windshield. Viper flinches but shoves the throttle to its max. The creature clings to the bug with the claws on each of its limbs. Others that hit the plow are pushed aside or under the vehicle. Lance can't tell how many, if any, are unlucky enough to have their heads squished. The ride becomes bumpier as the bug crawls over the still-living bodies of most of the scavengers. The first creature still holds on to the vehicle, its large golden eyes staring into Viper's soul through the thick glass. He shakes the dread he feels each time he sees a scavenger up close. The creature glances up and then begins crawling up toward the turret, leaving gouges in the windshield.

Lance curses under his breath then shouts back to Kingston. "Boom, you've got incoming from the roof!"

"Heard." Boomslang adjusts his position and sight. The creature crawls up onto the roof of the bug only to be met by a single shot through its lone weak spot. Bits of brain splatter across Viper's view. He flicks on the wipers, which just smear the blood, leaving streaks of white-red. He curses the ancestors that invented such a useless device.

Scavengers continue to be thrown or fall under the treads. A second later, the way is clear. "Status!" Lance barks over his shoulder.

"Clear here," Boomslang's voice comes back.

"I think we made it through. AI says we trashed two of them. Boomslang got four. Eight still up and regrouping. I don't see the others."

Lance nods even though there is no one to see him. "Time to get to safety." Even though they hadn't been able to get a brain or collect the bounty, they are all alive. That's all that matters.

"Viper, I have Gov on comms."

Lance doesn't take his eyes off the rocks and gullies that make up the landscape in this area. "What now?"

Oversight checks his screens. "I'm not sure, but it sounds like all the sat and sat navs are going down."

Lance blinks and takes a moment to process the new information. "How's that possible? They've been up since before the war."

Kingston shakes his head. "I get that. But that's the problem. Gov says a lot of the sats have already gone down and the ones that are left have been nursed to keep alive. Gov says they decided it was important to let everyone know now before everything goes completely dark."

"Shit. Without sat intel we are as blind as the nasties at night. How long until things go dark?"

"Have no idea. And Gov isn't saying. I don't think he knows either."

The day can't get worse, Lance thinks just as the bug hits a boulder and begins pulling to the right. Viper fights the joysticks to keep the bug straight. He's wrong; the day could get worse. The bug has broken a track. He guns the engine but gives up when the vehicle insists he go right in circles.

"What's the scoop, Chief?" Boomslang's voice comes from the turret.

Lance shuts the engine down and yells back. "Dead track. We're dead in the water unless you can fix it." Lance releases the clasp of the shoulder belt and, along with Oversight and Boomslang, exits the vehicles. He shrugs off the chill that runs down his spine despite the heat. They will have to reach shelter on foot. It won't be easy.

CHAPTER 3 - RYKER HORNE

Ryker Horne splays out on the ancient metal park bench and surveys what is his. There isn't much. Apart from the bench, which is missing a foot, he can count among his treasures an intact lamp fixture that he has no way to power, a piece of hard plastic pipe, a metal grill grate, and his locket. He pulls the small, tarnished object out of his pack and, careful not to injure it, opens it to reveal a small, faded picture of a blonde woman. Time and radiation have taken their toll. Even though it's faded and almost colorless, this small thing has somehow survived the war and reminds him of what it meant to be human before the war. It also reminds him of what they had done to him—both personally and to his group.

Humans had caused the war that had mutated him. He remembers the day when the mad president, unsure of winning another election, had ordered a nuclear strike on the protestors—in his own country. Ryker had been taking a shower in his home—where was it? it was so long ago—a city they had called Biltmore or something. The flash of light—the heat—the pain. He had survived as many had that were outside the blast radius. He had survived as many had, but the country did not and the world, his and that outside, were never the same.

Those that had survived had changed over time. His skin had peeled as if from a bad sunburn, in large dry flakes that sloughed off at regular intervals. His hair had been singed off. His fingernails had fallen out to be replaced by sharp, yellow talons. Then new skin had formed, different and harder. That's when the pain had been the worst. He had often thought of ending it then and there. He didn't understand radiation but he understood he would never be human again. He had often considered killing himself and ending the torment. Many had. Most had. But he was a coward. Others had chosen not to end their lives. Some were cowards, others just didn't care, and a few clung to hope.

Ryker places the small treasure back in the plastic pouch he wears around his waist. Those that were changed had learned over time, or because of it, that they didn't die, or maybe they just had an extremely long life span now. Many scavengers think it is the will of God that they suffer. He doesn't believe in God. He often wonders what kind of god would impose suffering of this kind—any kind—and for what reason. God hadn't done this. God hadn't caused this. Humans had. Humans who wanted more power than they knew what to do with and people who tried to stop them. Humans had caused the war and his suffering. He once cursed the humans who had taken away his humanity but now, years later, they are all dead. Now he curses the humans who are safe from the radiation and who bear the children who now hunt him and his kind.

Hatred had replaced his fear many years ago. There was no fear if you thought you were ageless and armored. Short of a freak accident or a human bullet through his brain, he cannot be killed. Some days he wishes he had a gun with which to kill himself; other days he wishes he had a gun to kill humans.

He pounces tiger-like off the bench and lands on all fours. He bounds out of the cave he dug for himself in the ruins of an old human city. Ryker stands on his legs and peers around the rubble that's showing signs of spring. The war had damaged more than just humans. He sniffs the air and scans the area. He had not been followed after his outing earlier that morning. Most of his kind run in packs. Ryker chooses to run alone. A pack might be stronger as a group, but a lone scavenger is harder to spot. He has to be more cautious. He was almost caught at the old ruin where the humans and the packs had fought. Ryker had gone out to explore an area further from his home than he had ever done. *I should have stayed to a place I know*, he grumbles to himself as he wishes he could remember what cool weather felt like.

He had already picked clean all of the normal places. Time and the war had left little to find. There was always the chance there were things further away. That's why he had decided to go out today. Then the humans were there. He kept his distance. He watched as a pack charged the armed men. They had run to their car—he remembered that word—then the humans had killed several of his kind. Ryker curses again as his claws find a rock that he hurls with all his might. "We are human—changed but still human." Ryker hates humans. Ryker wants to kill humans. It is the human thing to do.

CHAPTER 4 - LANCE

"Can you fix it?" Viper looks at the broken tread. Boomslang and Oversight are by his side.

Boomslang shakes his head. "Not unless you have a spare tread hidden away somewhere that I don't know of."

"I was afraid of that." Lance's mind races. His first priority is keeping his team safe. And safe now means somewhere deep and away from scavengers and radiation. The first he could handle. The second was questionable now that the bug was out of commission. "Boomslang, Oversight, we need to get to that shelter before the storm hits."

Oversight speaks up. "It's closing fast, Chief. I don't think we can make it before it hits if we're walking. Maybe we could dig the bug in."

"Not if it's a Force 7. Maybe with a Force 5 it might work, but even then it would be chancy. We need to get to that shelter. Grab all the gear you can carry and let's move out. The sooner we get there the safer we'll be." The three team members rapidly and efficiently pull everything that isn't attached out of the bug, which Lance seals with his passcode. He knows the bug still has electronics the scavengers could get to, but there's not much he can do now. Lance Garner's priority is his team, not the equipment. Gov would have to deal with any losses. "Direction?"

Oversight points toward a small rise. "45 clicks—about 30 miles."

Lance gives the signal to move out and the other two men drop in behind him as he jogs toward the mound. The rocky terrain makes progress slow. An hour later the group pauses to survey the area. The men breathe hard; Oversight is breathing the heaviest. "We covered five miles. At this rate we won't make it."

Boomslang pulls out a pair of field glasses and pans the area around the hill.

Viper's breath is rapid as he wipes sweat from his brow with a sleeve. He glances at the young team member and says, "We'll make it, soldier. Or do you want to fry out here?"

Oversight grits his teeth and then snaps to attention. "No, Sir. We will make it, Sir."

Lance grins. "I guess I should've known better than to pull rank on you." Even though he's the leader of the team, none of them hold any rank or are even in the so-called New Army. Their jobs for the Gov were freelance, as were all of those that were not responsible for patrolling borders and keeping the rest of the world out—not that any had ever tried to come in after the debacle of the war.

Deforest grins back and relaxes but turns serious again. "Humans weren't built for this heat and humidity. This is scavenger weather."

"I've got movement." Boomslang breaks into the conversation.

"Scavenger?" Viper's attention snaps back to his gunner.

"Multiples. Looks like it."

"Have they spotted us?"

"No, I don't think so—wait, check that. They've definitely seen us. I count seven. They're moving this way."

"Confirmed. Sat radar shows seven. What do we do? Run for it?" Oversight's rifle comes up to the ready position.

Lance glances around. "We stand here. We have the high ground. It's not much but it's all I see. Normally I'd say head back to the bug but, if we do that, the storm will definitely fry us."

Boomslang winces as he repacks the field glasses. "Not much cover here, Boss."

"I get that. But this way we get a chance to make for cover. Scopes up. Let's take out as many of them as early as we can. Make them all clean kills. No telling when we'll be able to get more ammo," he says, then adds to himself, "or if, with the sats going down." The team drops to a knee as one and snaps the long-range scopes up into position. It takes a few seconds for Viper to spot the targets. When he does he flips the zoom on the scope to maximum and shifts his aim to the lead creature's head. Tracking the loping scavenger is difficult but he manages to keep it aligned. "Fire at will. Good hunting." Viper watches the creature approach, timing its vertical movement. He holds his breath and squeezes the trigger. The sound of the rifle echoes around him and he is rewarded as the creature's braincase explodes. The creature continues to run, headless, and then stumbles and falls. Another one drops from Boomslang's shot. The scavengers behind the leader ignore their fallen comrades and run over their carcasses. A third creature drops, the victim of Oversight's bullet. Two more fall in rapid succession. The four remaining scavengers cut the distance separating Viper and his team and themselves in half when two more of them fall. Oversight's second bullet misses and whizzes past the head of one of the creatures to bounce off the armor of the one behind it. Viper aligns the crosshairs on one of the remaining attackers. He squeezes off the round and curses as the head bobs out of view as the scavenger changes direction to avoid a gully.

The three, seeing the scavengers are too close for scopes, drop them and start firing using the mechanical sights mounted on the barrels. The bullets all miss the vital spots and either bounce off the armor or rocks. "Two left!" Boomslang yells over the rifle fire. "Come on, you suckers! Meet your maker!" His rifle barks and splatters against the chest of one of the remaining creatures, which stumbles back from the impact but does not go down. The two creatures close the distance and leap up the mound. Kingston yelps as one of the scavengers takes a chunk of his vest with a swipe of a claw. Oversight slams the butt of his rifle into the head of the creature and flinches as blood and brain splatter across his face shield. The creature flails and then drops to writhe at his feet.

The remaining scavenger flings itself at Viper, who is knocked to his back by the impact. His rifle goes flying. Boomslang and Oversight spin to help their leader but neither has a clear shot. Viper grapples with the downward thrust of a claw that misses his neck. He brings a leg up to where the creature's groin would be but his kneecap smashes into bone armor, getting the worst of the impact. Pain shoots down his leg as the creature swipes at his face. He hears his teammates yelling but can't make out the words. Adrenaline floods his system as he smashes his head into that of the creature. Its yellow eyes blink and the creature pulls back, stunned for a second.

Lance's head slams again. This time the scavenger hisses through its saw-like but gapped teeth. Lance struggles against the still slashing arm with his. His other hand fights to reach the knife at his belt.

The creature's head splatters over Lance's face but the body continues to claw and fight for several seconds before it goes still. Lance pushes the carcass off him and struggles to his feet. He wipes his face with a sleeve then glances from the dead scavenger to his teammates. Lance stands panting, his body covered in sweat, the scent of the nasties' blood mixing with his own. "What took you guys so long?" The adrenaline washes over him.

Boomslang looks at the butt of his rifle, grins, and says, "You were having fun."

CHAPTER 5 - LANCE

Exhausted and pumped up on hormones, Lance orders, "Take a break. We've got a lot of walking to do." He drops onto the remnant of a large, concrete block. He pulls a ration pack, rips open the foil packet, and tips the liquid contents down his throat. He grimaces as the sour fluid hits his tongue. *Things that are healthy for you are never good,* he thinks. Boomslang and Oversight sit on the ground next to him.

"When do you think we'll be recalled?" Oversight asks. "We were due a month ago."

"Why do you want to be recalled?" Boomslang's question is gruff, as is his nature. "This is why we signed up, to kill nasties. To help humans take back what's theirs."

Oversight pushes a ration pack toward the large gunner. "Don't you get tired of it all? Don't you want to go home to your family?"

Boomslang rips the pack open with his teeth, spitting the foil onto the ground next to him. "I get tired, but I never get tired of killing nasties. We're the good guys." He pauses a moment before continuing. "'Sides, I don't have family—you know that—unless you two chumps count." Deforest turns his attention to Lance, who scans the area with a pair of glasses. "How about you? You get tired of this, don't you?"

Lance lowers the glasses. "Sure I do. We've been out in the field for longer than most teams. I want to go home. I want to live a normal life." He pulls an image out of his pack and focuses his attention on it. "And I do have family—beyond you two." He replaces the image, sighing. "But I have a mission. We all do." Viper stands and adjusts his gear. "Break's over. The sooner we get moving the sooner we can get to safety." Worry gnaws a hole in his stomach as he glances around.

The team resumes its march. "So why does Gov need an intact nasty brain, anyway?" Boomslang asks as the three make their way around an overgrown ancient park. After the war it isn't safe for human or nasties. "I would have thought there would be plenty of those around, given how many we've killed."

"That's the problem. We can't kill them unless we shoot them through the head or blow them apart. Hunters aren't known for finesse. We're all trying to survive, not take specimens," Oversight explains.

"So why do they need them?" A small, furry animal that could have been a cat in a former life scrambles out from under a large rock onto which Boomslang has stepped. His rifle snaps up but he holds his fire as the creature scampers for its life.

"They want to find out what makes them tick. We really don't know anything about the scavengers. We know they showed up after the war, but we don't know much else. Most of the science stuff stopped once the war broke out." Oversight sweeps a hand across the landscape around them. "And, as you can see, there's not much left. We humans are just trying to survive, not get smarter. I guess Gov wants to know if there's an easier way to kill them than shooting them through the head or wasting a bunch of munitions."

Boomslang grunts. "That would put us out of a job."

"I wouldn't mind." Oversight's response is subdued.

Lance, who has been taking the lead, glances back. "What about you, Deforest? Family? You got a mom, right? Anyone else?"

The team walks in silence crossing an overgrown stretch of concrete that may have at one point been a highway. It takes a while for Oversight's response. "Just my mom. She's real sick, though." His voice catches. "She's real old—not old enough to have lived through the war, but close."

"So why'd you leave her?" Boomslang asks, his voice less gruff than usual.

"She wanted me to join up. I wanted to stay and help her, but she said I was useless." Oversight's gulp is audible. "She said, 'Go out and learn to stand on your own.' She kicked me out of the house, said she wouldn't have a son who wasn't willing to be independent and stand up for himself." Oversight's voice trails off. "I did because that's what she wanted ... "

"Kid, that's rough." Boomslang kicks at a rock, one of many underfoot. "At least you have a mom. I can't remember my parents. I had them but they wanted to explore the country; they went into one of the rad areas. They never came out. That's what the Gov home said, anyway."

Oversight doesn't respond for a while as the three walk. He finally breaks the silence. "That's weird."

Viper's attention shifts laser-like to his comms guy. "What do you have? Targets?"

"No. No targets. But things are weird."

Lance relaxes but still scans the area, looking for any threats. "Weird?"

"Yeah. Normally comms are readable, but it sounds like it's fading or dropping out."

"Is that unusual? After all, we're out in the middle of nowhere." Lance continues forward.

"Like I said, weird. Usually the tech is crystal clear if the orders aren't."

"What's that mean? I mean, about fading?" Boomslang spits at a patch of green growth.

Deforest shrugs but the pack on his back makes it invisible. "Don't know. Like I said, I haven't seen it happen before."

"What's Gov say about it?" Lance asks.

"He says it's nothing to worry about—just the sats going down."

"That's something to worry about." Lance's concern is written on his face.

"If Gov says don't worry about it, then don't worry about it. Gov is always right," Boomslang says. Lance doesn't respond.

"Maybe it's just the storm," Oversight continues. "Not like I could do anything about it. This gear is old tech—and there isn't much new tech."

The team keeps moving forward, but Lance's mind races. In all their years together he's never heard Oversight complain about comms. Something is happening he has no control over. How would the sats going down affect the mission? How would it affect the team? He walks in silence. He is the team leader. He has to keep the team going and complete the mission. He can't shake the feeling of unease. Gov should have decommissioned the team, but the order to acquire a complete scavenger brain had come through. Now comms are acting weird—the sats shutting down. He leads the team in silence.

Several hours of hard walking later the team settles in for the night as the sun sets behind the clouds. The teammates stop in what they deem a defensible spot and unroll their packs. "I'm exhausted, tired, and hungry," Oversight grumbles.

"We all are. Get some rest." Lance settles down on his pack and stares up at the dark and murky sky. "Do you ever wonder about the stars?" he asks with a yawn.

"No. Why should we?" Boomslang's response comes from a yard away.

"I do." Oversight is sitting up on his pad looking out across the barren landscape. "I wonder what they are like. My mom used to tell me stories about how the sky was full of them before the war messed up the air. I wonder if they are still there behind the clouds."

"Yeah. I still wonder about the old stories—you know, about men walking on the moon." Lance rolls over onto his side.

"Why would anyone want to walk on it? It's just a fuzzy blob of light like the sun. You can't see either." Boomslang yawns.

"Don't you wonder what they look like behind the clouds—if the clouds weren't always there?" Oversight's question insists on an answer.

"Crazy talk. Knowing won't make it any easier killing nasties."

"Is that all you ever think about? Killing and shooting things?" Deforest lies down, his fingers laced behind his head.

Boomslang grunts, then says, "Mostly." He pauses, then continues. "Sometimes I wonder about the animals—I mean the animals that got caught in the war. I wonder what they think of us for destroying their world."

Lance grunts back. "It's not just their world. It's our world too—our country. Most of the world is okay, after all. When I get decommissioned, I plan on going someplace else to see what the country was like before the war. I want to see all the food and people and tech and not have to worry about looking over my shoulder wondering if a nasty is about to kill me."

"It'll just make you want stuff you can't have. What's the point?" Kingston asks, staring up at the darkening clouds.

Lance thinks a moment before answering. "Because I want something better. There must be more to this crappy world than hunting scavengers. I want to live in a world that's safe and makes some sort of sense."

"It doesn't exist. That's a dream. We live in the world we have and we just have to make the best of it. It's not that bad. We get meals—that's more than many people get—and we do something worthwhile—killing nasties."

"I guess you're right," Lance replies, but his tone makes it clear he doesn't agree.

"Of course I'm right. We're ridding the world of vermin. We're protecting ourselves and those we love. We're doing the patriotic thing. I know I'm doing something that's good and I'm good at. What else could anyone want?" Kingston yawns, then asks in a sleepy voice, "So, Oversight, did you tell your mom you signed up?"

"Yeah," Deforest sighs. "All she said was, 'It's about time.' I wonder if she really appreciates what I do and how much I've changed. I'm not the kid I used to be."

"I get it. But, like I said, you had a mom. I grew up with a bunch of other kids I didn't know or like for the most part. I got into a lot of fights—you know how kids are. And raised in a Gov home we grew up hating nasties." Boomslang thinks a moment. "Or maybe we were taught to hate them. I guess I don't know. Either way, I grew up wanting to join the hunters.

"Well, I didn't really want to, but I wanted to make my mom happy."

"I just wanted to make myself happy."

"Are you?" Deforest asks.

"Happy? Nah. It's work. I guess I didn't think killing nasties would be so hard. It sounded like it would be an adventure—you know, like stories people tell. I didn't count on having to sleep in an ancient junk pile." Kingston guffaws in the dark night. Then in a subdued voice he adds, "I can't say I'm happy. But I'm satisfied. My life could be a lot worse."

"Yeah. I agree. But don't you wish you had a family? Someone to settle down with? Live a normal life?"

"Nah. How normal of a life have any of us had after the war? This, what we do, is normal, at least for me. The only person I have to take care of is me—and my team. Yup, it's not a bad life. I'm satisfied."

Lance hears Kingston yawn and roll over. This wasn't the life he would have chosen for himself, but he wasn't sure what he would have otherwise picked. That's why he wanted to go somewhere where life was closer to what it was before the war, someplace where scavengers didn't roam. Mostly he wanted to go to wherever Roxy was.

CHAPTER 6 - LANCE

Lance lays back staring up at the dark gray night sky, his hands folded behind his head. Thoughts race through his mind dancing from topic to topic, future and past. The night is as silent as it is dark apart from the occasional stirrings of nocturnal creatures that scramble across the debris fields. Lance, certain the perimeter alarms the team had set up will alert them to any scavenger or large predators, relaxes. He tries to peer through the clouds to see the stars he knows are there but he has never seen.

His first team leader, Jim, had often told stories about the stars and how humans had reached the moon. Lance sighs, wishing he had paid more attention. A hard knot forms in his stomach as an image of Jim's face forms in his mind. The image has faded over time, but the smile remains as clear as if Jim were standing in front of him. A grin forms on Lance's face then vanishes as he remembers what he'd done. The scavengers had come out from behind the rocks. It was Lance's third encounter. He'd convinced himself he'd done well on the first two but now he knew that was a lie. Panic had gripped him as he fired at the creatures' onrush. The scavengers had outnumbered them three to one. The team had fought the onslaught, cutting down a few of them. Then Jim's rifle had jammed and he'd been overwhelmed by four of the nasties. Jim had knocked one of them away with the butt of his rifle, but the other three had thrown him to the ground. Lance's throat tightens as he relives standing frozen as one of the creatures had sliced into Jim's throat. Jim's scream had turned to a gurgle.

Lance slams a fist against the ground as tears form in his eyes. He'd stood and done nothing as the nasty had killed Jim and wiped the smile away. Rage had consumed Lance and he splattered the remaining scavenger's brains across the landscape.

My hesitation cost Jim his life. I failed him. Lance cries into a sleeve so as not to wake his team. Gov had promoted him to team leader based on the testimony of the team's comms member and recordings. Lance hadn't wanted the promotion, but Gov had insisted. He'd been punished for his mistake. He'd been given more responsibility for not living up to his responsibility to save Jim's life, or so he believed. When he'd finally given in and accepted the promotion, he vowed to himself to never fail his team the way he'd failed Jim. He vowed to never accept more responsibility. Lance lay deep into the night listening to the sounds and trying to imagine a different life. He felt things were failing, more than just the sats.

CHAPTER 7 - LANCE

Viper snaps awake and fully alert from a restless sleep. The perimeter alarm they had set up before camping had gone off. The high, distinctive chirp might be confused for a strange bird, but to Viper and his team it means trouble. He glances around in the darkness, making sure Boomslang and Oversight are up. They are. Oversight's visor is down. Viper asks, "What have we got?"

"Five heat signatures. Maybe more. Coming in from the northeast. Sat is weird again."

"Stay on top of it. Let me know if things get worse."

"Will do. They aren't moving this way. I don't think they know we are here. It looks like they are just roaming around, scavenging I would guess."

"In the middle of the night?" Boomslang's rifle is at the ready, his scope down.

Oversight shrugs in the darkness. "Either that or they're lost."

Viper speaks up. "They're probably just going somewhere and ran across something interesting. It's worth a look. Scopes down. Boomslang take the left, Oversight right. You know what to do. Stay out of sight and don't do anything stupid." Viper has given the same orders numerous times, but his team knows what they are doing. It is a habit he can't seem to break. On some level it's more of a reminder to himself than to his teammates.

The three move silently through the dark night. The ever-present humidity clings to them the way their sweat-drenched clothing under their body armor clings to their skin. The team spreads out as they approach their target. Viper's bud crackles and Boomslang's voice announces, "Contact. Five nasties. If they're scavenging they aren't doing it now. They're heading south as a tight cluster. What's the word, Boss?"

Viper winces. "SH-2, stay with comms protocol."

"SH-1, this is SH-2. What the hell do you want us to do?"

Viper grins despite his annoyance. "SH-3, do you have contact yet?" Lance's bud clicks once. Oversight isn't one to waste words. Viper asks, "Any chance we can grab one for its brain?"

Two clicks from Oversight. "Not unless we cull the herd first," is Boomslang's response.

Lance doesn't want to engage if he doesn't have to, especially at night. Getting a brain for Gov is important, but keeping his team alive and safe is more so. Wiping out another group of scavengers wouldn't make much difference. "SH-2, SH-3, pull back. We can hunt when the odds—and the light—are better."

One click from Oversight. "But they're here for the picking." Boomslang's voice is almost a whine, then he adds, "Roger. Pulling back." There's disappointment in the voice of the large gunner.

Lance turns back toward their campsite as Oversight's voice startles him. "SH-1. Nasties have changed direction. Heading your way. Repeat. Nasties coming your way. One minute." Viper's rifle comes back up and he snaps the scope down. He peers through it. Living matter shows up as a dark purple against a black background, spots of purple he ignores. Those are plants and small animals. Several seconds later a large moving blob appears. He keys his bud. "Contact. You guys around?"

"Now who is breaking hunter protocol?" Boomslang's voice holds a chuckle.

"I could use some backup if you guys aren't sightseeing." Viper then adds, "SH-2 and 3."

One click from Oversight. One click from Boomslang. Viper continues sighting through the scope, waiting for the large purple blob to resolve itself into separate images. That would be the indication they were in range. He toggles his bud. "SH-2 and 3, I guess we have a party. Take 'em as you get 'em. I don't feel like spending the night with a bunch of scavengers." The response comes back. Click. Click.

Viper watches as the large purple blob breaks apart the way he imagines a living cell would. A moment later one of the targets falls. His bud yells at him in Boomslang's voice, "One down!" Viper will have to have a talk with his gunner. Another scavenger goes down. No clicks, no Boomslang. That was Oversight. Viper lines up a shot on the largest and closest blob, holds his breath, and squeezes. The muzzle flash lights up the area in front of him, but he only sees the purple blob in his scope collapse. He'd heard stories of the ancient days when people played games where they killed things. He couldn't imagine having such a luxury, but he could imagine it would be something like this.

That was three down—two left. "Take the lead down. Let's see if we can get a brain from the laggard." Click. Click. Viper lines up another shot even though he knows his team can take care of it. He squeezes the trigger and the lead blob drops. *Now what?* he thinks. Gov hadn't told them how to get the brain without shooting a scavenger through it. The blob disappears. The creature is too close. He flips the scope up and is met with the night. He stares down the mechanical sight, but only sees black. "SH-1, 2, do you have a shot?" Click. Click click. "Boomslang, take it. I don't know how we're supposed to get a brain, especially at night." Just as he finishes the order a large, dark shape crosses his sight. He shoots. A moment later a dark form lands a foot in front of him. Viper, his heart pounding, shifts his aim to where he thinks the head of the nasty is. The shot misses as the creature's hard body leaps. An instant later the creature lies dead at his feet, its cranium shattered, the gelatinous fluid pouring onto the ground in the light of Viper's lamp.

"Bingo!" Boomslang's exclamation echoes in his bud.

"SH-3 to SH-1. You okay?"

"Yeah," Viper responds, fighting to still his nerves. "A bit rattled, but in one piece," he admits. "Back to camp. Let's try to get some sleep." Viper nudges the scavenger with a toe. The creature remains motionless. "I wish I knew what makes your kind tick. Too bad we had to waste your brain. I wonder if you know how much trouble you cause us." Lance shakes his head in the darkness, then turns and heads back to the campsite.

CHAPTER 8 - LANCE

"Here." Boomslang tosses an object at Viper's feet. It gives a small bounce and rolls toward him.

Lance picks it up. "What's this?"

"That's what the nasties stopped for. An old plastic bottle."

"Did it have anything in it?" Lance shines his lamp into the dusty interior of the container.

"Doesn't look like it. I guess they just wanted it. I don't get them. It's not like the world isn't littered with those things—one of the few things that outlasted the war."

"Should we go search for their cache?" Oversight asks, dropping to sit on his bedroll.

Viper shakes his head. "Not worth it. Every one we've come across is just bunch of rocks and a collection of the useless stuff they've scavenged. Grab some rest while you can." Lance lies down on the bedroll and rolls onto his side. "Besides, we have the rad storm to worry about. Get some sleep. Morning will be here before you know it."

Deforest picks up the plastic bottle Lance had placed next to their rolls. "The old world threw mountains of these out, I hear. And they are still here. More humans were killed in the war than there are bottles still around."

Kingston grunts from the ground. "What's that supposed to mean?"

Deforest flings the bottle into the rocks behind him. "I don't know. It just makes me feel small and insignificant somehow, you know? The bottles are more significant than we are, it seems."

Lance stares up at the sky, thinking about bottles and the stars he has never seen. Minutes later Deforest's steady breathing and Kingston's heavy snoring tell him his teammates are asleep. He lies awake, wondering what Deforest's mother will think once the team is decommissioned.

What will Kingston do? *He'll probably sign up for another sting,* Lance thinks. He knows what he will do. He will go home and apologize for running out.

CHAPTER 9 - RYKER

Ryker's head snaps toward the sound. The shot echoes across the landscape. He ducks behind the burned-out shell of an ancient vehicle he had long ago determined held nothing worth taking. Another shot rings out. His pulse races and his eyes scan the litter-strewn yard. He spots movement at the top of the rise a hundred yards away. Three men—stupid men for they were in the open—weren't shooting at him but at something on the other side of the mound. Maybe they are the same three he saw earlier. *It doesn't matter who they are. They are focused on whatever is happening on the other side. This will be easy.*

He lopes up the mound, staying low and shifting direction to make himself more difficult to hit if spotted. His claws make clicking sounds as they hit the ground and various objects in the yard, but unless the humans are listening for him his movements are silent. The crack of rifles continues, the three men firing oblivious to his approach. He has to move fast if he is to take all three. It would be difficult but not impossible. He has to make sure an alarm isn't raised until it's too late.

Ryker inhales deeply and steadies his nerves. He's a dozen yards behind the trio hidden behind the remains of a rusted metal girder. He pounces. He spins the closest man around. The man's eyes grow wide in surprise then quickly turn from terror to horror as Ryker slices his neck open. The body drops to the ground, spewing blood. One down, two left, but the sound of his attack and the body falling have drawn the attention of the other two men, who whirl around. Seeing their spasming comrade, the two bring their rifles up and fire without aiming. Ryker lunges at the closest human, a bullet flying off Ryker's armor. The man is thrown onto his back, expelling his breath in a loud "oof." Ryker can't see the man's face with the hat's shield in the down position, but he can see his neck. A quick swipe of his hand and the man struggles no more.

Bullets are now continually bouncing off his back armor. Ryker ignores them. They will do no damage unless they hit his head. He pulls himself up to his full height and faces the remaining man. There is terror and panic in the man's face, which had drained of blood. He is young, his red hair a mess of strands under his hat. He fires the rife without aiming, too terrified to remember to hit Ryker's head. Ryker takes a step forward and the young man yells as if to make his aim more accurate, the bullets more effective. Ryker hisses and moves forward. The human panics, takes a step backward, and trips over a large hunk of metal to fall onto his back. Ryker moves to stand over him. The man expends his clip against the large plate of armor at Ryker's chest. A ricochet fractures a rock that sends a splinter against the hapless man's face, drawing blood. He drops the now useless rifle by his side.

The man's terror is palpable as he screams, "I give up! I give up! Don't kill me! Please!" Ryker stands over him, catching a glimpse of the name tag on the man's chest, which he can't read. The human's eyes are as large as plates but Ryker has no use for plates. An instant later the plates are gone, replaced by a bloody gash that runs from ear to ear. A second later and another gash appears across the man's neck.

Ryker steps back and surveys the bloody scene and himself. Apart from a few new nicks that will heal over time and splatters of human blood, he is unhurt. The same cannot be said of the three men who lie in pools of their own blood. Ryker knows he's been lucky. Had the men seen his approach he probably wouldn't be alive now. He doesn't enjoy killing, but killing humans is necessary in order to survive. He moves from body to body, taking what is useful. The rifles he leaves; he can't use them with his claws. His own armor is as good or better than that of the humans. He leaves that. A few things he keeps, such as the belts. He collects them, not as trophies, but to secure the bits of his home together. Whatever small objects and trinkets the men had he can trade with other scavengers. The electronic gear he destroys. None of his kind knows the codes to enable the devices—they had tried over the years. Some of his kind think the electronics are keyed to the people who use them. No human had been caught alive to say one way or another.

Satisfied he had picked everything of value or use, Ryker turns his attention down the hill. He lopes down its side and stops short. Five scavenger bodies lie lifeless among the mound's debris. The brains of each had been opened by the humans' rifle fire. If any of his kind had survived, they were long gone. Rage and hatred fills Ryker at the sight of the bodies before him. *How could humans kill us so callously?* he thinks. *We're human too. It's not our fault.* He glances back toward the group he overwhelmed and is glad he killed the three who had killed his kind. Vengeance feels good. The skin on his face tingles. A storm is coming.

CHAPTER 10 - LANCE

Lance trudges through the hot rain. He glances at the sky, but there is no sign of the rad storm, just the gloom of dark, ever-cloud-covered skies. He curses the clouds, the darkness, the rain, and mostly his inability to control his own life. His teammates distract him.

"So why do you hate scavengers so much?" Deforest asks, turning to Kingston as the team slogs forward.

The gunner shrugs, readjusting the grip on his rifle. "Everyone hates scavengers."

"Yeah, but for as long as I've known you, you seem to have something personal against them." Lance pauses, considering how to phrase what he is about to say. "You seem to go out of your way to kill them."

"Nasties are terrible. They're taking our land and killing us."

"You're still alive. You never said you wanted land."

"That's not the point."

"What is the point, then?"

"Look. They're inferior to us. They aren't as smart. They're animals. Who cares if I kill them?"

The three men walk in silence, each busy with his own thoughts. Oversight breaks the silence and whispers loudly enough for Boomslang to hear, "You apparently do."

Boomslang grabs Oversight's shoulder and whirls him around to face him. Oversight's eyes grow wide in surprise. Boomslang yells, "Listen! I grew up with no parents in a home full of kids just like me. We were taught to be patriotic and fight for what is right. We were told scavengers are the enemy, that they made the world poorer and worse after the war. I'm doing what is right. I kill nasties because they need to be killed. If we don't kill them, they'll kill us. I don't need anyone to question my loyalty!"

Oversight's hands go up, palms forward. "Okay, okay. Relax! I never said you were disloyal. I was just wondering, that's all."

Lance steps between the two men, separating them, then turns to Boomslang. "Stand down! No one questions your loyalty or ability. But as long as you're part of this team"—he turns to Oversight—"you'll both get along and act as a team. Like the team we have been, are, and will continue to be." He lowers his voice. "We all have our reasons for being here. What matters is we work as one so that we can go home after our hitch is over."

Boomslang grumbles under his breath while staring at the ground. He looks up and shoves an outstretched hand to Oversight. "I'm sorry I got upset. I—I just want to do the right thing. Friends?" Boomslang's eyes plead.

Oversight nods and grasps the gunner's hand in his own. "Don't worry about it—friends. We've been friends ever since we met. I'm sorry I upset you. I—I was just curious, that's all."

"Okay," Viper moves to the front again. "Now that that is settled, let's get to shelter."

The three continue to walk for several seconds. Boomslang speaks up, his voice tinged with sadness. "I wanted to do the right thing. That's why I signed up. Growing up I never measured up to the other kids, especially the older ones. I was always getting into trouble and usually got caught. The house masters kept telling me I was worthless and would never amount to anything or be smart enough to do the right thing. Everyone there was told becoming a scavenger hunter meant doing the right thing. All the kids I grew up with became hunters. I—I wanted to be like them so we all signed up together." Oversight isn't sure how to respond and remains silent. "I thought I could prove to them I had changed. I was responsible. I could do the right thing."

Oversight asks, "Did you—prove it to them, that is?"

"I don't know. I've never gone back since I signed up. I don't think I want to go back. It's just a place of bad memories for me," the large man admits. "I'm not even sure I have anything to prove to the masters—they probably don't even remember me now. It's been a long time." Boomslang drops into a heavy silence.

Lance glances over his shoulder at the gunner as he walks. "If it means anything, I don't think you have anything to prove to anyone. You're a good person and a good friend."

Boomslang swallows. "Thanks. That means a lot. You're a good friend too—and I'm really sorry I snapped."

CHAPTER 11 - LANCE

"Take five minutes," Viper orders. They've been walking for several hours, the rough terrain making the journey longer than it should have been. Luckily, they haven't crossed paths with any scavengers but there has been one group on the horizon. Lance drops and sits on a boulder, pulling the water bottle from his belt. He takes a swig and keeps his gaze shifting around the area. There's no sense in letting their guard down. Boomslang and Oversight are arguing about something trivial. He lets them. Life is stressful enough without having a way to vent frustrations and fear. Unless things get physical, he won't intervene. He can't afford the same luxury of blowing off steam. Instead he pulls a picture out of his pack. It's worn but sealed so it won't deteriorate. The process had cost him a week's worth of chips. The woman who looked back at him is smiling, her red hair short with bangs. Her green eyes peer at him as if she is standing in front of him. How long has it been? A year? Ten? It is hard to tell. Time isn't something he cares about when hunting. It is a temptation that distracts him with hope things will end or get better. Lance knows things will end when he is either dead or decommissioned. He will do everything he can to avoid the first and only Gov knows about the second. Roxy had insisted she go with him, help him hunt. But he had told her in no uncertain terms he wouldn't endanger both of them. She had pleaded. She had threatened. She had cried. He had never seen her cry before. In many ways she was the stronger of the two. He'd run out on her in the middle of the night to sign up. He'd hoped she'd understand. Sighing, he repacks the image. "How far to shelter?"

"We have trouble." Oversight breaks into Lance's reverie.

"Nasties?"

"No. At least none that I can see. That's the problem. The sats are going down. I've got maybe two sats I can connect to. And the sat data are coming in sporadically. Most of them are garbled. What I can make out I wouldn't trust without corroboration."

Lance curses. "How about comms to Gov?"

Deforest toggles the now useless shield up to the hat. "Nothing but static. We're on our own apart from a data feed or two."

"Maybe Gov will find a way to reactivate the sats or get another comms signal out." Kingston kicks a rock for emphasis.

Viper's mind races. "I make shelter still 35 clicks. How far is the storm?"

Deforest shakes his head. "Closer—how close I don't know. I'm blind."

Viper stands and adjusts his pack. "Break's over. Let's hustle. With any luck we can beat the storm. Eyes sharp! We don't have Oversight's. We don't want to be ambushed by nasties." Boomslang and Oversight drop in behind him and continue the trek to the underground shelter. Lance knows finding it blind will be nearly impossible, but he doesn't say anything. He scans the horizon looking for scavengers. Being blind unnerves him. He's certain his team feels the same. The sats had always been there, always seeing what humans couldn't, for hundreds of years if the stories were to be believed. *How did people survive without sats?* he wonders. The scavengers did, but they were deadly and didn't have any predators apart from the hunter teams. A movement at the corner of his vision brings his rifle up instinctively. He relaxes when a small, rodent-like creature runs past, one of the mutant variety. It isn't worth the effort or ammo since it is harmless and inedible. Not knowing where the enemy is makes him jumpy. He wishes he were a sat up high. Lance pauses and looks up at a mound of old-world debris. "There." He points at the hill. "Let's get to high ground and see what we can expect. It's only a couple hundred yards and shouldn't delay us much." Viper knows any delay can be deadly but he will feel better having some eyes instead of none.

"Someone had a party," Boomslang announces, surveying the dead scavengers that litter the ground around the team.

"Another team must be in the area." Viper shoves a decaying carcass with his boot.

"Maybe we should group up. The more of us there are the better our chances." Deforest's voice cracks with tension or fear. Lance can't tell which, but he gives Deforest the benefit of the doubt.

"No can do. Gov says teams of three, no more, no less. Don't want all of us to be wiped out by one of the larger packs."

Boomslang snorts. "We've never seen one. Largest pack we've seen is 30, and that one was easy-peasy."

"Don't get cocky. We had a tough time with that one." Lance recalls the incident. It had been a vicious fight with the scavengers coming from all sides. They had been lucky to survive.

"We did fine. If we can handle twenty-five we can handle 30." Boomslang always thought he was good. Viper knows he is, but that certainty has made Kingston rush into questionable and dangerous situations. Lance decides not to argue the point. Instead he motions to the top of the hill with his rifle and the team follows.

"Shit! What happened here?" Kingston stares at the three bodies the team finds at the top of the mound.

"They must've been overrun." Deforest's face is a pale shade of green-pink.

Lance grits his teeth as he holds his emotions in check, then stoops and rips the name tag off each body in turn. He hands one to Boomslang and one to Oversight. He doesn't consider burial. It is a waste of time and hasn't been practiced since the war. There is more land than humans, and whatever God there was before the insane president pushed the button had been destroyed in the blast. The tags work as a reminder of those who had been lost and as motivation to stay alive and to hunt until decommissioned.

Kingston stands, examining the bodies. "They weren't overwhelmed. A single scavenger did this. I mean they weren't overwhelmed by a group." His voice holds awe and surprise.

"Are you sure?" Lance moves next to his teammate to peer at the rocks.

"Certain. There is only one set of claw marks up and one down." The gunner points at the chipped and scratched ground free of debris.

Lance examines the single set of clear claw marks dug into the ground. Something seems wrong, but he can't put his finger on it. Oversight draws his attention.

"Guys." Deforest's voice is more question than statement. "I think I saw something over there." He points at a group of large, rusted, metal girders at the bottom of the mound that thrust up toward the sky like bony fingers out of the earth.

CHAPTER 12 - LANCE

Lance's scope comes up. He scans the ancient debris. "I see three nasties. Grouped. They haven't spotted us."

"Easy-peasy." Boomslang's rifle is up as well.

"Too far. Besides, our mission is to get an intact brain, remember? We don't have time with the storm coming. We need to get to shelter while we can." Lance lets the rifle drop to his side. Boomslang grumbles but lowers his to a ready position.

"I agree with Viper. I'm blind. I've never been blind and I'm not afraid to admit it scares the shit out of me."

"Maybe comms came back," Kingston suggests, dropping behind Deforest as Lance leads the team down the mound.

Oversight's face shield drops down for a moment then flips back up. "Nothing but static and noise. We're alone. Gov isn't going to rescue us any time soon. I have a feeling they have bigger problems than just the sats going down." Lance throws a questioning glance at his teammate but says nothing and gets no answer.

Lance surveys the route before them. The carcass of an ancient building stands in the open plain. Crumbling girders and hunks of rusted and decayed metal are more skeleton than structure. He doesn't see anything inside to cause worry but the hairs on the back of his neck stand. He shakes off the feeling and says nothing.

The three file down the slope. Lance isn't used to being blind. He depends on good intel to make good decisions. Without one he doesn't have the other. His muscles feel tight as he walks. Tension is something they deal with every time they encounter the nasties, but now being out of contact is making him nervous and alert. He tries to slow his breathing and ease the stress in his body. Kingston and Deforest are talking about the team they had come across. It hadn't been the first, and it won't be the last, but this one is different. The two comrades' voices are low and their tone concerned. "How could one scavenger kill an entire team?" Deforest asks.

Kingston's response is measured. "It couldn't. Even if it got one of the guys the other two would have taken it out. It was probably a pack. Nasties don't run alone."

Lance wonders what they had missed examining the site. The claw marks still bother him but he can't say why. The uncertainty grows in him as he glances around. There are the bodies and multiple tracks along with the dead scavengers, but only one set of tracks going out where the other team had been killed. Maybe the rubble had shifted and destroyed the other tracks. Boomslang's yell brings him back to the present. "Nasties behind! Four!" Viper's rifle comes up as he whirls to face the threat.

Four scavengers rush in their loping gait toward the team. "Why didn't we see them?" Viper yells as his scope snaps into place and he targets the lead creature.

"We're blind, remember? They must've been in the building somewhere," Kingston replies as he fires off a shot. It goes wide as his target swerves. He curses and lines up another shot.

Deforest's face shield comes down, then an instant later it flips back up as he remembers his displays are useless. He sights his rifle manually and squeezes off a shot. A scavenger's brain explodes in mid-lope and the creature tumbles neck over heels.

Lance catches movement at the edge of his vision to the right. He glances and sees five more scavengers rushing their position. "More company! Four o'clock! Count five!" He swivels and fires off a shot that takes out one of the creatures at the edge of the pack. The rate of fire from the team increases as the scavengers close in. Several more go down in quick succession.

"Bring it, you muthafuckers!" Boomslang yells as he foregoes his scope and begins shooting the creatures that move too close to sight with a scope. His first shot hits its mark.

"Watch your backs!" Lance barks, then a moment later he commands, "Hand-to-hand." He lets the rifle drop to his side and grabs the pistol and knife from his belt. He curses and wonders how they could have allowed themselves to be trapped so easily. His pistol barks and the scavenger that has leapt at him falls to the ground, its head pierced by his bullet. Three creatures are left in the secondary pack and all are rushing him. He reacts instinctively and ducks as one takes a swipe with its clawed hand, missing him. Lance fires but the bullet bounces off the scavenger's shoulder plate. He stabs upward with the knife, which elicits a scream of pain from the creature as he makes contact with its head. The scavenger, not realizing it is dead, redoubles its efforts and the scream turns to a hiss as it bowls into Lance, pushing him to the ground. The other two creatures fling themselves at Lance to aid their wounded companion. Lance screams, his mind going red as he lashes out with his knife. His legs push the first creature aside before the other two reach the team's position. Lance is too busy with his own problems to hear the yells and gunfire coming from his teammates. He manages to get to his feet just as the second creature throws itself at him. A shot from Boomslang's rifle forces the creature back as its head bursts into a shower of blood. Hissing, the first scavenger faces Lance but likewise goes down.

Lance turns to thank Boomslang but is horrified to see the last of the creatures fly onto the big guy's back and slash with an arm. Viper's pistol snaps up and, without thinking or aiming, Viper fires off a shot. Time seems to slow for him as the bullet hits its mark, but only after the claw slices a portion of Boomslang's arm the way a turkey would be carved.

Kingston screams in pain, rolling away from the dead creature. He writhes as blood gushes out of the long, jagged wound. Deforest's face blanches white, his breath rapid, but he reaches back and pulls a white box out of his pack. He tosses it to Lance, who kneels next to the wounded teammate and begins administering first aid to him. Lance curses as he helps Deforest staunch the flow.

CHAPTER 13 - LANCE

Half an hour later Kingston is sitting up, the gouge in his arm sanitized and sealed. The pain pills have brought clarity back to his eyes, but Lance notes the gunner won't be much help in another firefight. "Are you okay?" Lance asks.

"Yeah, fine. The wing stings a bit though."

Lance nods. "Can you move it?" Boomslang lifts his arm a few inches then bleats as the pain overrides the pills. He drops the arm down by his side. The gunner is sweating profusely. "We have to get you to meds. That scavenger took a huge chunk of your muscle and you need to get a regrow."

"I'm fine. Don't worry about me." The sweat on Deforest's brow says otherwise. "Damn animals! I'll teach them to mess with humans."

Lance shakes his head. "Don't be a hero. You're useless to the team. You can't use a rifle and you know it. We need you patched up and operative. But our first priority is to get to shelter before the storm hits." He glances at his watch. They had lost time during the fight and getting Boomslang mobile. "If we hustle, we may make shelter before it arrives." It's a lie. The team heads down the hill, Deforest now bringing up the rear. Kingston, with the help of the pills, moves rapidly, but his arm hangs limp at his side, his gun slung over his good arm. Lance glances back at his friend's face. It is drawn and tired, but Kingston manages a grin at him, which he returns but doesn't feel.

Lance focuses on scanning the area and making sure no other nasties surprise them. *Shit. I should've known better. It's my job to make sure my team survives. I've let them down. I should have been more alert, more cautious,* he thinks and then curses himself. *Being blind is no excuse for getting the team hurt. Now we're down one man for all intents and purposes. I have to get them to shelter. After the storm passes, I have to get them to meds and have Boomslang brought back to speed. Shit! This isn't going to be easy. I need eyes. I need support.* He knows each team is on its own and, now that the sats are down, the only eyes he has are those of his team and himself. He kicks a rock out of his path in frustration and is glad when neither Deforest nor Kingston start a conversation. He's in no mood for banter. He notices the brim of his hat deepening in color.

CHAPTER 14 - RYKER

Ryker spins at the sound of gunfire in the distance. His skin prickles and the air smells acrid. It's a sure sign a storm is coming and, from what he can tell, its a large one. For a moment he considers returning home, then he decides a chance to kill humans is more important. The storm won't get here any sooner. Over rubble and debris he lopes toward the sound of the battle. A minute later he is in sight of a hill. Three humans are being overrun by nine of his kind. There will be nothing left of the humans and there is no sense in him taking any of the salvage. He would have helped if the humans had outnumbered the scavengers. He turns and runs in the direction of his home and safety from the coming storm. He stops and flinches. His skin burns. He has never felt a storm that had that effect. For a moment he thinks he's sick, but he shakes the thought off. He has survived many storms and is immune to normal levels of radiation, but there is no sense in tempting fate. He resumes his trek back to his sanctuary. The sound of rifle fire continues, then stops. He pauses, confident the humans have been wiped out. It has been a good day to kill.

He takes a different route back in order to climb the hill he had been on earlier. Ryker wants to check the strange object he had spotted when the humans had interrupted his search. A couple of minutes won't matter. He clambers up the mound, searching for the object. He finds it: an intact solar cell buried among the rubble. His claws carefully excavate the black rectangle from the surrounding debris. The wires are gone. The glass is intact, but scratched and dirty. *Still*, he thinks, *beggars can't be choosers*. He pockets his find and searches the area for an additional minute, but finds nothing else. Still, this is enough and will bring food for at least another day or two. He again starts down the slope and stops at the decaying remains of three scavengers. He rifles them, taking anything of value. He finds a hunk of shiny metal not worth carrying, a plastic bottle—he could use that—and a pistol. He examines the weapon. It's useless to his kind; the mutation had seen to that But it could be worth something. Ryker wonders where the now dead scavenger had found it. He shakes his head in a human manner. The mutants must have been desperate to have attacked. Three on three at range is bad odds when facing rifles with scopes. Even five on three is a chance not worth taking. They had bet. They had lost. He is still alive. He is the winner.

If he ever comes across those who had done this he will make them pay dearly. *Humans are animals*, he thinks. His skin prickles. He stares up at the dull sky that he had never seen so angry. He shivers despite the heat, then runs.

CHAPTER 15 - LANCE

Lance drops to sit next to Deforest. Boomslang has gone off to relieve himself. Kingston glances over at the team leader. "We aren't going to make it, are we?" His voice and expression are somber. He glances up at the dark night sky. "How can we get to shelter without wheels?" He points a thumb back in the direction of the vehicle they left behind. "It's not like Gov will help us now. We're going to die, aren't we?"

Lance remains silent a long moment as he considers the best way to respond. "We'll make it. But, no, Gov won't help us now that the sats are down. The only way we'll fail is if we give up. I'm not saying it's going to be easy. It's a long hike, and who knows what we'll run into along the way? But if we stick together and remember we're a team, we'll make it. I know we're all tired—I'm tired. We should have been decommissioned long ago but we have a mission. We have to do what we can and stay alive until the day comes—and it will—when we get pulled back."

Deforest interrupts. "But with the sats down Gov won't be able to tell us we're decommissioned. How will we know? We could be out here hunting scavengers for the rest of our lives."

"Gov has always come through for us. He'll find a way to get word to us. He wouldn't leave us hanging." Lance doesn't feel confident and knows deep inside he's lying, but he has to keep the team together. He has to keep them safe. He has to keep them alive. The only way he can do that is if they stay together and look after one another. "Don't give up on me. We're a team. Gov takes care of his own."

Deforest glances over at Lance. "Maybe we were decommissioned already. Maybe we should be home by now."

"Maybe." Lance's voice turns firm. "But we have a mission and until we get word either way, that's what we're doing. We can't afford self-doubt." Viper stands, his voice firm. "Is that clear?"

Oversight blinks in surprise. Viper rarely yells. Kingston nods. "I know. I haven't given up. I just wonder how we'll get to that shelter without help."

In a quiet voice, Lance responds. "Together."

CHAPTER 16 - LANCE

He pushes the team as fast as he can without breaking them. They're exhausted but they would be dead without shelter. Lance wishes he could let the team rest and relax but they can't afford the time. They had earned rest—long ago—and kept earning it. They deserve better than having to hunt scavengers in this hellhole of a country. They deserve to be home with their families and loved ones. Lance trudges in the lead and wonders what it would have been like had he grown up without a family or any real friends. What if he had been raised to hate and hunt scavengers like Boomslang had been? Well, he hunts them, but it is a job. He has no feelings one way or another toward or against the creatures. They are just the mission—or so he tells himself. He knows the creatures are trouble and will kill humans on sight, but Lance doesn't know whether that is because it is in their nature or because humans hunt them. Up until the sats had gone down humans had had a distinct advantage. Now, he isn't so sure. Despite the old-tech rifles, humans are still outnumbered and have to live in barricaded enclaves. Scavengers roam at will across the land, what is left of it after the war. Lance wonders about other countries. He has heard of them but, as far as he knows, they don't interact with either the humans or scavengers. Lance's country had become a country non grata since the insane president rose to power and had destroyed it. Lance pushes on and he pushes his team. He curses the president long dead, the scavengers, the land, and himself.

CHAPTER 17 - RYKER

Ryker slows as he approaches his home. It doesn't pay to be careless. He scans the rocky outcropping for humans or scavengers. Seeing none, he moves down the ridge and enters the pile of rocks that is his dwelling. He drops the treasures he had found on a small pile of other objects he can trade for food. Some scavengers seek objects. Some seek favors. Some seek food or shelter. He has no need for human objects. He has no need for favors or companionship. He has shelter, but finding food is difficult for both scavenger and human. He drops on all fours, facing the entrance to the outcropping that is his shelter and home. He had smoothed the ground with his own claws and hands.

His skin still prickles. The storm nears. He'll be safe, but humans will need to seek shelter. He knows he can defend his home from scavengers and has done so, but humans seeking his home as a shelter, humans with rifles, would be something else. There is no other way out apart from the entrance he watches. The acrid smell in the air tells him the storm is going to be big—bigger than most. He shifts uneasily on the hard ground and wonders if he should find someplace safer and more sheltered. He sits a long while as the prickling of his skin increases. Other storms had set the skin under his armor tingling, but not like this. The sensation makes him want to rip the chitinous scales off, but that is impossible. He stands on his feet, glances at the small stash of treasure near the back of his home, and then decides it will be safe during the storm. He runs out of the entrance. There is a human ruin; he had stumbled on it during one of his forays. He had explored it and discovered it was empty, but there had been signs humans had been there in the past. He'd found a shaft to an underground level that would serve as shelter until the storm passed. He hadn't gone down, but he guessed it was some sort of storage facility.

Now, with the storm, he knows humans will find shelter with their own kind. He'll be safe at the ruin.

He climbs the ridge and surveys the area. There's no sign of humans or other scavengers. The sky has turned green and dull and the air is as humid as it always is, but the tingling of his skin tells him remaining outside might be fatal. The human area is a day's travel from his home. He sets out at a run. He'll outrun the storm.

Ryker runs fast and strong, avoiding larger obstacles while leaping or scrambling over smaller ones. He feels alive when he runs. His heart races and the air moving across his face and unarmored hands brings back memories of running in the backyard as a child so long ago. He jumps the wreck of an ancient rusted bench and scurries up a hill of broken concrete and twisted metal overgrown with the stunted vegetation that passed for plants after the war. He remembers the bright green color of grass and the bright colors of flowers. Now the plants are a dull white green and what flowers they produce are tiny and unimpressive. Ryker misses the world of his childhood.

CHAPTER 18 - RYKER

Ryker looks up at the sky. The rain spatters against his face and drips down the sides, washing the dust and grime away. It's a warm rain. It's always a warm rain. He lets the water clean him, relaxing in the sensation of the drops striking him. His mind goes back to a time long ago.

The world is white and cold. He remembers staring up at the gray sky and frozen rain floating down onto his tongue. He remembers the things humans called clothes—a lot of them. His memory looks at his small hands wrapped in gloves to keep them warm. The snow comes up to his waist. He had slogged through it in the backyard, leaving a snaking trail behind him. He'd gone further from the house than he'd ever gone before. He'd turned back and his house was gone. Fear had gripped him. He had cried, his tears freezing on his face. He was cold. He was lost. He was afraid. He wanted to go home. He wanted his mother.

Not because he knew what he was doing, but because the trail he had made was the easiest route through the deep snow, he ran crying, retracing the route he had taken. Several moments later he rounded some trees and caught sight of his house. He rushed home, ran through the back door and into his mother's arms.

The warm rain continues to pour down on him. Ryker's attention comes back to the present. He had forgotten about the incident over the years. He had forgotten the fear and had forgotten the world could be something other than gray, wet, and humid. Ryker runs through the rain, trying to shake the feeling of fear and loss.

CHAPTER 19 - RYKER

Panting, Ryker scrambles up the old girder and surveys the area around the depression he's in. The human shelter is nearby but he hasn't been there in over a year. The exact location is a foggy memory. He also wants to make sure there are no humans in the area. He has no desire to fight when the storm is so close. The landscape is typical of the area after the war. It's hilly and pockmarked with slabs of old concrete and asphalt. Crumpled ancient buildings have fallen into their component parts apart from the occasional clump of corroded girders. But the most prevalent thing that clutters the landscape are the plastic bottles and small electronic components encased in plastic that have fallen and disintegrated, leaving the plastic.

There are no humans or scavengers that he can see. The air smells sharp, acrid. Ryker doesn't remember anything about the area, but he's certain he is on the right path. A movement on the far horizon catches his eye. It's fast. *It must be one of the human machines*, he thinks. It's too far away to worry about, and he's too far away to be noticed. Ryker climbs down the girder. He sits against it and pulls a bit of moss from his pouch. He chews on the hunk of food, bland and tasteless as all food is now. He has even lost the memory of taste over the years. He often struggles to recall what peanut butter was and how it tasted. He does remember he liked it when he was small, and what it was called. He remembers the smooth texture, not the grainy, dry, and grassy texture of the moss he now chews. He remembers the color—a light golden brown. But the smell and flavor of it are beyond his ability to recall. Ryker remembers flavor was something wonderful, always different, exciting, and sometimes horrible. He wouldn't mind tasting something—anything—even something horrible. It is all the same after the change.

Ryker spits the moss out more in frustration than disgust—after all, it provides the nutrition that keeps him alive. *What is the point?* he thinks. He packs the remainder back in his pouch and sighs. He starts down the path of debris he knows will take him to the human shelter.

CHAPTER 20 - RYKER

Ryker crouches on a large outcropping of twisted and rusted metal. Night has fallen and although he has spent the day running, he hasn't come across either more of his kind or humans. His skin prickles under his armor. His face itches but he doesn't scratch it. Instead, he peers into the gloom and darkness, getting his bearings. He's almost there at the entrance to safety. A small part of him feels unease. He hadn't seen signs of humans the last time he'd been here, but he hadn't gone down into the black shaft. There could be humans below ground. He recalls the place below his home as a child, even though he doesn't remember what it was called. The place was scary when he was young. *Now I'm powerful*, he thinks. Ryker knows some creatures lived underground. He doesn't fear creatures. They are small and no match for him. Only the humans with their guns are a deadly threat. The echo of a sound off in the distance startles him. He stares into the night but sees nothing and the sound doesn't repeat. Ryker's stress and anxiety don't go away. The itching persists as well. Ryker rubs his face with the back of his hand. He squirms on his perch, knocking a pebble, which clatters to the ground below. He knows the storm is growing. He'd been near others and felt their effect on his skin. But he'd never felt one with this unrelenting intensity. Fear runs through his body—or maybe it is a rad wave—he doesn't know which. But he knows he has to reach safety regardless of what lies underground. He ambles down into the night, away from the approaching storm.

CHAPTER 21 - RYKER

Ryker has traveled for most of the day when he stops to scour the area. He stops and searches for something edible, having eaten the last of the moss. He realizes he might be in the human shelter without food for an extended time and needs enough to get him through. He feels the storm is close, stronger than any he had encountered. There would be nothing he could eat in the shelter. He digs around in the rocks, gravel, and debris. The distant sound of human weapons fire attracts his attention. Cursing to himself, he jumps in surprise and caution but relaxes when he sees the humans on the horizon, far outside the range of their weapons. He resumes his search, finding an ancient key, an empty plastic bottle, and the remains of a corroded battery, but nothing edible. His skin stings incessantly now and the pain is becoming unbearable. He decides he has wasted enough time. He has to get to the shelter. He has to either find something edible there or do without until the storm passes.

He sprints in the direction of the entrance. He remembers the location; the area now looks familiar. The opening is easy to find on top of a lone hill. There's an overgrown rusted sign by the entrance. Traveling as fast as possible, he soon comes in sight of the hill. He's almost there. The sky begins to shimmer, the green tinge wavering as the rad storm approaches. He pushes himself faster, wanting to escape the storm and the pain under his armor. He scans the hill to make sure no humans or scavengers are in the area. He isn't sure what he would have done had there been any. *With the huge storm this close, I have to find shelter deep underground*, he thinks. Fighting will delay him and expose him and anyone else to a painful death.

CHAPTER 22 - LANCE

The team slogs through the muddy puddles and drenching downpour. The warm rain does little to help their spirits or visibility, so Viper sets a slower pace despite his better judgment. They have broken camp, tired from the interrupted night. Kingston and Deforest are chatting about something inconsequential, but Lance's mind is elsewhere. He is home.

"Why not? I'm as good as you when it comes to taking care of us." Roxy's voice has a sing-song quality he can rarely resist. This is one of those rare times.

"Because what would happen if we were on the same team and you got killed? How do you expect me to go on knowing I let you die?"

"Who says you'd be the team leader? Lots of women lead hunter teams." Before he can reply, Roxy rushes onward. "And I wouldn't let you die." There is the sense she wants to add a "Harrumph" or "So there!" but her lips are set in a firm line, leaving the words implied. "Aww, come on," she implores. "We'd be together at least."

"There's no guarantee we'd be assigned to the same team," Lance argues.

"There's no guarantee we wouldn't be."

"You just like arguing."

"No, I don't." She grins, but Lance remains strong.

"I don't want to lose you. I don't want you struggling and killing things. I want to keep you safe so we can start a family when I get back."

"I'm a better shot than you are." He couldn't argue with that. She was. "You never said you wanted a family." Her voice softens but the determination in her face remains.

He had never thought about having a family, at least not until he had blurted it out. Now he decides he wants one almost as much as he wants to protect humans from the scavengers. "Well," he stumbles over his words. "I do when the time's right. When I'm done with my tour."

She pulls him to her and looks up into his eyes. "Okay. We'll have a family—after we get back."

Early the following morning, Lance gets up before Roxy wakes. He stands watching her sleep, her breath regular and easy. He leaves a note and sneaks out. He had signed up for a tour as a scavenger hunter and knows she will be mad as hell. But that will pass and she will understand him and the logic of it. At least he hopes she will. A year later he is promoted to team leader when the previous one is killed. The memory of the promotion stings even to this day. He hadn't deserved it. He'd failed to protect Jim. He wants to get home to Roxy. He wants to start a family. He wants to be decommissioned.

"You okay?" Boomslang jerks Viper backward from a sheer drop where a stream, formed by the rain, ran.

"Uh, yeah. Thanks." Viper snaps back to reality. Sheets of rain strike his face and run down his neck under his clothes and armor. They will dry quicker than he will once the rain stops. "I guess I was thinking about stuff." He glances at his watch. The rad storm would be on them in a couple of hours. The rainstorm and his darkening hat brim are just an appetizer, a precursor of the radiation wave that will hit them. "Let's hustle. We still have a long way to go to find that shelter. The sooner we get there, the better I will feel." He glances back at Oversight and Boomslang. Kingston's face is as drenched as he imagines his own to be. Deforest's visor is down and the rain sheets off the copper-colored plastic resin. "Anything from Gov or the sats?"

Oversight shakes his head. "Not a chirp, beep, or ping."

"They must know we can't talk to them, right?" Boomslang asks.

"Oh, I'm sure they know," Oversight responds, "but I don't think they can do anything about it. Sats are old tech. We lost the capability to fix or send up new sats. We're lucky we could receive from them as long as we did."

"Do you ever wonder who Gov is?" Lance suddenly asks as he resumes the trek.

"What do you mean? Gov is Gov, isn't he?" Kingston asks, confused.

"Yeah, but who is he? Where is he? Deforest, you talk to Gov. What's he sound like?"

Deforest shrugs as he follows behind Lance, the rain bouncing off his shoulder pads. "Just a normal guy, I guess. Doesn't have much chitchat or a sense of humor, but people are like that."

"One day I'd like to meet him and have a long talk about things."

"What sort of things?" Deforest asks.

"Oh, I don't know. Like why we haven't been recalled yet. Why he let the sats go down."

"Like I said, old tech. We don't have resources to build new ones. Nothing lasts forever, you know," Deforest explains.

Lance remains silent, but thinks, *Neither do we*. His foot splashes into a puddle and he almost loses his balance. He recovers, cursing. "I almost broke my fool ankle. Keep sharp, team. I don't want to have to carry one of you the rest of the way—or you me." He plows through the rain down a long hill. Boomslang and Oversight follow close behind.

An hour later the rain stops and Viper calls a break. The sun is at its highest point behind the murky and roiling clouds but provides little additional light. The team clusters on a huge slab of ancient concrete as they devour their meal. Lance scans the area, remaining alert with his weapons close at hand. Fatigue is setting in. There is little conversation as they eat, the previous night and the downpour wearing the three down. Lance walks off to relieve himself, grabbing his rifle as he goes. The ground is littered with debris, remnants of the ancient world with scattered puddles of rainwater. Having completed his duties, Lance heads back to his team but pauses by a large puddle. He glances down at it, surprised by the reflection that stares back at him. It's not the one he remembers. The face that examines him through the ripples is older, grayer, heavier around the cheeks and jaw. He recognizes the eyes despite them appearing more tired. He pulls his hat off and runs a hand through his hair. There's less than he remembers.

Lance straightens with a long sigh. "When did I get old? When did I have time to get old?" He heads back toward his team but glances back at the puddle.

"Move out," Viper orders as he returns. He checks his watch, then asks, "Are we still heading in the right direction?"

"Straight and true," Oversight responds, glad at least the compass built into his visor still works. The team packs its belongings and the three resume their journey. Their progress is faster, but the oppressive humidity makes breathing a chore and their breathing is labored. The terrain remains a series of rolling debris hills, concrete slabs, and puddles. What vegetation they come across is insignificant and struggles to survive. The team walks for an hour without encountering any living creatures. Lance pauses to wipe his forehead and scans the horizon. He adjusts his pack and continues forward. The coming storm makes the hairs on his neck stand, giving him the illusion he is being watched. He shakes off dread, knowing it's just the heightened electrical charge prior to the radiation wave. He doubles his pace.

CHAPTER 23- RYKER

Ryker scans the area again. He sees no humans, no animals, and none of his kind. He sniffs the air, the acrid scent is stronger, the prickling of his skin now a stinging. It's annoying, not painful, but the storm will be larger than any he has ever experienced. He has to get to the shelter. He runs down the hill and is only minutes from his goal when a sound to his left draws his attention. Ready to escape, he circles the hill and spots a pack of four scavengers rummaging, apparently oblivious to the coming storm. His stomach rumbles. He has to get to the shelter, but the need for food is immediate and there is no telling how soon the storm will pass. There is no guarantee there is anything edible in the shelter. He has to eat now.

Ryker rummages through his pack and with a claw pulls out a rusted tin can. *It should be good for a bite*, he thinks. He approaches the pack, can held in front of him, making enough noise to not startle the scavengers. The five, hearing the tumbling pebbles and click-clack of his claws against the debris, look up, ready to run or attack, and then relax. Despite the fact he looms over them in size, they feel no fear. There are five of them and only one of him. Each, seeing they are safe, goes through their pack and pulls a piece of salvage. Ryker goes to each in turn, looking at the offered objects. Most of the scavengers hold items that are inedible; one holds something that looks like green moss but is actually mutated grass. Ryker offers the can to the one who holds the moss. The creature takes a step back, declining the trade. Ryker takes a step forward, his opposite a step back. Ryker takes a step back and places the can into his pack, digs a moment, and pulls out the useless pistol. He takes a step forward. The scavenger places the moss on the ground and Ryker imitates the motion. He then stabs the moss with a claw and walks backward with his prize. His opposite grabs the pistol with a claw and places it into its pack. The trade complete, Ryker scuttles away down the side of the hill and heads toward the refuge.

He stops some distance away, scans to see if the pack is following him, and, sure that he is safe, settles down to consume part of the green mat. It is dry and flavorless but provides enough nutrition to sustain him for a few days. Ryker tries to remember what real food tasted like before his change, before the world became the drab gray all around him. It had been too long ago. His memory fails to recall any of the flavors of his youth. He sits for a long time, trying to recall. He remembers something called ice cream, and white-and-brown balls of cold, but for all of his trying the flavors escape his will and memory. Ryker stands and continues his journey to shelter, running to dissipate some of the pain and frustration of having lost so much. He pushes himself and runs bounding, leaping, and striking the ground claws first, each impact driving the claws into the cluttered ground. He runs, imagining the ground to be the humans who had started the war, those who had changed him, and those who now hunted his kind. He covers a lot of ground, but the route is roundabout and snakes beyond the area he knew packs held as their own. There is no sense trespassing and perhaps being attacked. He is certain he will reach the safety of the shelter without inviting danger or damage to himself.

He stops and peers at the large mound in the distance in front of him, his destination. The air is still acrid, and his skin stings continuously and at random spots under his armored plates. His face itches, but he learned long ago, at the cost of a large scar, not to scratch it with his claws. Instead, he rubs it with the back of his hand, but the itching persists. He gives up and pushes on. The storm will hit soon and he will be safe. Then he can rest.

CHAPTER 24 - RYKER

The scavenger lies face down in the dirt near a muddy stream beside a tall collection of steel girders and concrete blocks. Ryker moves quickly to its side. *Maybe there's something worth taking,* he thinks. He pulls up short when the creature's hand twitches. Its left leg is bent at an angle it should not be able to form. Ryker approaches with caution in case there are others around—or humans. He hears the injured scavenger's rasping breath. Ryker reaches the creature's side and looks down. The armor around the creature's hip is shattered and exposes the flesh underneath. Ryker glances up at the girders then at the creature beside him. The back of the head is bloody. The creature moans.

Ryker reaches down and rolls the scavenger over onto its back. The creature's face is old—old for a scavenger, but not for Ryker. It is an old human face. The face that looks up at him is scarred, wrinkled, and dirty. Its eyes pierce into Ryker's, pleading. Its breath is ragged and rasping. Ryker stares back, wondering what he should do. He has no medicines or even the rare herbs some of his kind use to treat problems. Ryker glances around and spots a large chunk of concrete. He scurries over to it and grasps it between his claws. He moves back to the injured scavenger, holding the weapon firmly. The injured creature's eyes dart from the rock back to Ryker's face. There is terror. Ryker raises the concrete high. The creature on the ground makes a strangled sound, its eyes wide.

Ryker cries. The pain burns. It stings. It hurts. He looks down at his knee, red, raw, bloody. The wound is ragged and speckled with bits of dirt and gravel. His bike lies on the ground next to him. He hurts. He is afraid. He wails. The warm sun beats down on him. Several moments later his mother rushes out of the house; the screen door slams shut behind her with a metallic ka-chink. She grabs Ryker up in her arms and makes soothing noises as she carries him inside.

She sits him down on the edge of the old kitchen table. She moves away, but quickly returns with a white box. Ryker's mother cleans the scrape while talking to him. Her voice soothes and calms him, so he stops crying and merely sobs. She applies an ointment that stings, but his mother's voice distracts him from his pain. She applies a bandage, then hands him a piece of candy. He smiles up at her and is then quickly wrapped in her embrace. She pats him on the head and tells him everything is okay.

Ryker flings the concrete aside. The wounded scavenger looks up at him, questioning, but still terrified. Ryker has no white box, no candy. He rummages in the pouch at his waist and pulls out half of what remains of his food and water. He places it on the ground next to the creature. He pats the creature on its head with a claw. Satisfied he has done everything he can, Ryker lopes away toward shelter, leaving the old scavenger alone. Ryker moves quickly until he is out of sight of the one he has helped. He stops and sits on all fours. He cries, tearless.

CHAPTER 25 - LANCE

They approach the body of the scavenger. It doesn't move. "It's dead," Deforest announces. The creature's eyes flutter open, dart from one to another of the team, then settle on Lance, who is the closest of the three. A chill passes through Lance as he looks into the eyes filled with fear.

"Shit!" Kingston hops back. He relaxes when the creature closes its eyes again and doesn't move. "It's still alive." He moves closer and raises his rifle at the creature's head.

Lance grabs the barrel of the weapon. "No! Leave it alone!"

Kingston glances at the team leader, surprised. "Why not? It's a nasty."

"It's already dying. Leave it alone."

"Then I'll put it out of its misery and we can get the brain Gov needs."

The rifle comes up with Lance's hand still on it. Lance pushes the muzzle aside. "I said leave it alone. We're low on ammo. Besides, look! The brain's damaged." Viper's voice is firm as he points at the pool of blood soaking into the ground under the creature's head. The scavenger, unable to understand the conversation around him, lies staring, its eyes wide and unblinking.

Kingston steps over the scavenger. "What's this?" He kicks a lump of moss and a plastic water bottle away from the creature. He turns back to Lance. "I still think we should kill it. What if it has friends?"

"If it has friends, maybe they won't attack us if we let this one live," Lance rationalizes.

The injured creature's eyes close; it exhales a long breath and lies still.

"Nasties don't have friends. They aren't human." Kingston spits at the creature. The wad hits the scavenger's chest plate. Lance throws him a critical glance but says nothing.

Deforest leans down and examines the creature. "It's dead. What should we do with it?"

Lance stoops and looks at the scavenger. "Too bad we couldn't salvage the brain. That would at least have given its death some meaning." He stands. "Nothing else we can do here. We should keep moving."

The team leaves the corpse. Viper leads, his thoughts conflicting with his emotions. In all of his years as a hunter, he's never considered scavengers capable of feelings or being afraid. They had always attacked and only stopped when they were dead or retreating. Now he had seen one, its fear evident and its eyes pleading. He knows it would have attacked them were it healthy enough to do so. Lance also knows he would have killed it as he has killed others of its kind. He had stopped Boomslang because he had felt pity for the creature. Lance doesn't like the contradictory thoughts and feelings he is experiencing. Uncertainty as a scavenger hunter is a luxury he can't afford—and it could kill him.

CHAPTER 26 - LANCE

Lance drops onto the ground after calling a quick break. His feet are sore. His back aches. His mind is filled with worry.

Deforest checks his rifle and then his pack as the three sit on a hill overlooking the skeleton of an ancient city now a pile of rubble and girders. "I'm running low on ammo." He checks their supplies and then tosses a fresh clip to Boomslang. "Here you go. You need any, Lance? I have one clip left."

Viper checks his rifle and pistol, shaking his head. "No, I'm fine." He has three rounds in the pistol and four in the rifle, plus a couple of clips in his bag. "You keep it. I guess we should call for a supply drop." He glances around the open but high ground they are on. "This is as good a spot as any. Oversight, call it in. We probably need some more food packs as well."

"Will do." Flipping his visor down, Oversight is silent a long moment, then raises the visor before speaking to Viper. "Done. It should be here within the hour. It took some retries to get the signal through, though."

"Is it still breaking up?" Viper asks. "I don't know what's going on, but it's probably not good." Viper pulls out a pair of field glasses and scans the remains of the city.

"Yeah. It seems to be getting worse," Oversight replies.

"Did you check with Gov? Did he have anything to say?"

"No. He must be busy with something. I'm sure he knows. I got a ping back that he got my message."

"Good. I'm sure he'll straighten it out." Viper places the glasses back into his pack, but his stress levels rise. Gov rarely ever only pinged back. "Nothing going on down there that I can see. I'm sure there are nasties there somewhere, but with the storm we can't afford to take a detour to find out." Lance pulls off a boot and knocks it against the ground. Dust and a small pebble rain out. His feet ache, his legs ache, and he hasn't had a bath in months. "May as well relax. It will be a while before the drop arrives. How are you holding up, King? We'll be cutting it close."

"Good as can be expected. I'm sore from walking and tired of eating jelly water all the time," the large gunner grumbles. "I can't remember the last time I had real food."

"Me either," Oversight chimes in. "I remember my mom's cooking. It wasn't much, what with the war and all, but it was at least solid."

Lance nods. "Last good meal I had was the night before I left Roxy. It was her birthday. We wanted to celebrate so we went out to one of those food stalls. I blew a month's pay on two pieces of real beef. She'd always wanted to try it and I figured it would be a good present." Lance winces at the memory. "I'm not sure I'd eat it again. I'm not sure she would either, but she was excited to try it."

"Yeah, I hear everyone ate beef back then." Kingston rubs his shoulder where his pack strap had chafed. "They were big animals, bigger than a man. I saw pictures."

"Believe me, it wasn't worth the money. I know Roxy pretended to like it, but I could tell from her face she was just making sure she wasn't being ungrateful."

"Do you ever wonder what scavengers taste like?" Viper and Oversight stare at Boomslang in disgust. "Yeah, me either." He chuckles. "Give me a solid ration pack or even beef any day."

"I'm not sure they would taste any better," Lance snorts. "Ration packs, jell or solid, don't make you gag."

"So what's the first thing you're going to do when we get decommissioned?" Deforest asks.

Boomslang responds first. "I'll sign up again, I guess. I might take a week to sleep and eat first. It's not like I have anyone or anything to go back to. The home has no one left that I knew. They all either shipped out or went somewhere else."

"No friends?" Oversight asks.

The large man's voice is slow and sad. "Nah. You guys are the only friends and family I have." He catches himself, then adds in a more chipper tone, "Who'd want to visit you two after spending years with you?" He sniffs. "You smell bad."

Oversight throws a ration pack at the gunner, who catches it with his good hand, rips it open, and downs the contents. "I'll go home back to my mom. She's really old now. I hope she's proud of me. I'm a bit nervous about that," he admits. He then adds, "I'm not signing up again. Once is enough. I'll stay home and take care of her. How about you, Lance, any plans?"

"I'll go home to Roxy. It's been long enough that she's probably forgiven me for running out like I did. I'll settle down and have the family I promised we would."

"No place to have kids, this." Deforest sweeps a hand across the desolate vista.

"I know, but we both want a family. It will be nice to not have to keep looking over my shoulder wondering if a nasty has my number."

Deforest grunts an affirmative then glances at his watch. "Drop should be overhead in a couple of minutes."

Lance stands and stretches, glancing at the clouds. "Get ready to grab it and move out. By the looks of the sky, I'd say the rad storm is closing in fast if our brims are any indication."

The team gathers their gear and Viper pulls the field glasses out once again. He scans the sky and horizon ahead of them. "Things are nasty up top. The clouds look like no storm I've seen. This is going to be a bad one and we're moving into it. The sooner we get to that shelter, the happier I'm going to be." Viper pauses. "Got it. Drone incoming." Another pause. "It's on track. Set up the pinger." Viper continues to watch the black dot resolve into a finned craft against the blue-black clouds as Oversight pulls a small silver-colored box out of his pack, places it on the ground, and taps a button on its side.

"Pinger active. Stand back. You don't want to get hit by the drop," Oversight announces. Viper lowers the glasses long enough to take several steps back then raises them again. The gunner and comms move away from the transmitter.

"It's about one minute out," Viper announces. A second later, "Shit!"

"What's wrong?" Boomslang asks, taking a step toward Viper.

"The package dropped."

"What do you mean dropped?" Oversight asks.

"Just that. It released over that city somewhere."

"Why would it do that?" Boomslang peers at the hill of debris in front of them.

"Maybe another team's drop?" Oversight asks.

"I don't think so. What are the chances a team would call in a drop around the same time we did in the same area?" Viper lowers his glasses. "Pretty slim, I'd think. Besides, look." He points straight up at the drone that flies, buzzing like an angry bee, directly overhead. "It's ours without a doubt." The drone fades into the clouds at the horizon as does its buzzing.

"Shit! Gov screwed up," Lance grumbles loudly enough to be heard.

"Now what?" Boomslang adjusts the pack on his back so it won't chafe his shoulders.

"We go after it. We need those supplies."

Oversight glances at the clouds. "What about the storm?"

"We move fast."

CHAPTER 27 - LANCE

Lance, Deforest, and Kingston's entrance into what remains of the complex half an hour later is uneventful. Deforest asks, "How much further?"

"Another click, I'd guess. It came down among a cluster of metal girders. It should be easy to find. Let's hustle, team." Lance clambers up a steep hill using his hands and feet. Boomslang and Oversight follow close behind. Lance's mood lightens as they close on the drop point. "We'll be good until after the storm with this drop," he says. At the summit, they stand and survey the area around them. "There!" Lance points to a group of tangled metal shafts thrusting up out of the ground toward the blue-black clouded sky. The three men slide down the debris side by side, knocking rocks, plastic, and shards of metal down in front of them as they go.

Another half hour later the three approach the drop point. "Why do you think it dropped here instead of at the pinger?" Boomslang asks.

"The sats have been acting weird. My guess is that had something to do with the miss," Oversight explains.

"One hell of a long miss," Boomslang grumbles.

"Hold!" Viper holds a hand up. The team is within a hundred yards of their target. "Shit! It looks like someone beat us to the package. Cover!" The teammates drop flat on the cluttered ground with their rifles on their shoulders.

"I count four," Oversight announces.

"Same here," Boomslang confirms.

"Same. Standard deployment. Move!" Boomslang moves to the left on his belly. Kingston goes right. Viper crabs up the center. Viper keys his bud and whispers, "Make it count. We don't have bullets to play with."

Viper's scope comes down and he focuses on one of the four images. "I have the middle two."

"Left is mine," Boomslang's voice whispers back.

"Got the right," says Oversight.

Viper whispers, "Take your shots as you find them." He holds his breath and squeezes the trigger. One scavenger down. He shifts his focus as the leftmost one falls as well. He lines up his shot and fires again. His second round misses. He curses. The scavenger on the right drops in a rain of splatter. The remaining creature runs but is brought down before Viper has a chance to aim.

"That's four down," Boomslang's voice crackles in his ear.

"Thanks," Lance sighs. "Group up but stay alert. They may have friends." Lance stands and scans the area before moving toward the bodies and the plastic crate that was their target. A moment later the three stand over the bodies.

"Stupid nasties," Boomslang spits. "What do they need with ammo?"

"They don't." Lance responds. "They're after the food packs." He kneels down and pries a plastic pouch from the claw of one of the dead creatures. He stands and tosses the pouch to Boomslang. "Food is scarce for all of us. Let's get the supplies stowed and get going." He glances up at the sky, the hairs on the back of his hand standing on end. "Storm's almost on us."

CHAPTER 28 - LANCE

A dozen yards from the drop point, things go wrong. "Get them off me! Get them off me!" Deforest's yell grabs Viper and Boomslang's attention. Despite each of them fighting off a scavenger of their own, they back toward Deforest's position as they fire point blank at the creatures attacking them. The bullets ricochet off the armor but, being at point-blank range, they manage to slow or stun the scavengers.

They had been walking along a gully when the pack of seven had surrounded and ambushed them before the team had time to react and find a spot they could defend. Kingston had managed to take out two of the scavengers, Lance one, before the remaining four were on top of them and the team was forced to fight for their lives.

"I'm out of ammo!" Deforest yells over at Viper as he reverses his rifle and slams the butt into the head of the creature in front of him. The scavenger yowls in pain, falls back, and clutches at its shattered head as it collapses onto the ground. "Get them off me!" Deforest yells again as he fires his pistol in rapid succession at the two nasties. One nasty drops on the ground next to him.

Lance aims and shoots at the head of the creature charging him. Blood splatters from the creature but the scavenger's momentum carries it past Lance, who steps aside. The headless body collapses several yards beyond. He turns and sights the creature that has knocked Deforest to the ground, its claw poised over his neck. The bullet strikes the back of the scavenger's head, splattering brain and blood over Oversight. The creature struggles a moment then collapses on top of the comms man.

Deforest groans, pushing the corpse aside. Lance grabs his hand and pulls him to his feet, asking, "You okay?" indicating the rifle. "What happened?"

Oversight holsters his pistol and retrieves the rifle before he answers. "Yeah, a bit shook up, but okay. Out of ammo."

"I'm out as well," Kingston confirms as he removes an empty magazine.

Lance checks his weapons. His voice is grim. "I've got three. One in the rifle, two in the pistol. Anything left in your packs?" He checks his own and his concern grows as the two teammates report he has the last of the ammo. "Shit! Here." Viper pulls a clip out of his pack and tosses it to Oversight. He hands another to Boomslang. "Now we have one clip each. Make them count. Let's hit the drop and see what goodies they gave us."

Kingston walks among the scavenger corpses, checking the small plastic pouches they each carry. He tosses the contents of the last pouch aside in disgust. "Nothing but useless trash. I was hoping we'd get lucky and find some ammo."

"That would be dumb luck." Lance wipes the scavenger's blood and brains from his face with the back of his arm. He won't smell better because of the encounter, but he knows he probably won't smell worse. He can't remember the last time he took a real shower. They always considered it lucky when they ran across a stream that was clean enough to wash with even though they couldn't drink from it. "I hope the shelter has showers. We need some luck, dumb or otherwise," Lance grumbles. "Without sats or Gov we have to make our own luck." He glances from Kingston to Deforest. His men are worn, dirty, and haggard. Their faces are smeared with dirt and scavenger remains despite their efforts to stay clean. Their eyes appear sunken and furtive. Lance walks to them and places a hand on each of their shoulders. "Hang in there. We're almost there. We can hunker down and get some rest until the storm passes." *But,* he curses to himself, *we need to go home. We've been out in the field too long. I want to go home.* To the team, he says, "Let's get going. We'll find ammo in the drop."

A few minutes later they come upon the cache. Deforest rips into the container then curses. He tosses packs to the other two team members.

"Where's the rest of the ammo?" Kingston asks, staring at the three packs of meals and two ammo clips in his uninjured hand.

"That's all there is," Deforest replies.

"Did the nasties get it?" Lance catches a ration pack.

Kingston shakes his head. "It doesn't look like the ammo pack was opened."

"Shit," Deforest curses.

"Gov really screwed us, it seems. The sats must really be causing problems for him. Don't waste what we have. I don't see us getting any ammo until after the storm passes, unless we get lucky and the shelter has some. And I don't expect more drops from Gov now that the sats are down," Lance grumbles.

CHAPTER 29 - LANCE

"How much further?" Kingston looks up at the sky with a worried look. "The sky looks too black for my liking." He's breathing heavily and he's walking slower than normal.

Lance points ahead. His arm aches. His entire body aches and he just wants to sleep. "It should be just beyond that rise. Yeah, this is going to be a nasty one. No telling how long it's going to take to pass, but it will be a while. I'm glad we got the drop when we did." He glances over at Oversight. "Once we're underground, any way of knowing when the storm has stopped?"

Deforest shakes his head. "Without sat intel, the only way I know of is for someone to stick their head up and take a look-see."

The gunner snorts. "Well, I'm not volunteering. I don't feel like getting my brains fried or ending up like one of the nasties."

Lance considers a moment before speaking. "We'll figure something out. We can always stay under a full week before coming up. That should be long enough. I've never heard of a storm going longer than three days. At least we won't need ammo while there."

Kingston grunts. "That doesn't sound like much of a plan."

"It's the best I've got without sats," Lance replies honestly.

The team continues its journey to the shelter. They scan the area around them as they move as quickly as the terrain allows. Occasionally Lance glances at the sky. His nerves are on edge and the air causes the hairs on his arms to stand on end. A hot, humid wind has begun to blow across the landscape. The three start up the rise Lance indicated. Unlike the surrounding area, the hill is spotted with patches of a dull, gray-green growth that struggles to come up in the cracks of old concrete, bits of broken asphalt, metal, and plastic. Lance breathes the wet air; his breathing is labored, as is that of his teammates. Deforest's sudden scream of terror rips at Lance's heart and stomach. He pivots, his rifle coming up quickly, in time to see the ground give way and Deforest disappear into it. Lance dives headfirst and tries to grab the man but is too late.

Lance, now on his stomach at the edge of a funnel-shaped hole, peers down into the darkness. "Deforest, you okay?" he calls into the blackness. He flips on the lamp on his hat. The dull, cream-colored beam illuminates the narrow shaft. Oversight is on the bottom, alive.

"Yeah, I'm fine—a bit banged up, but fine. I'll be sore." Deforest stands up from the rubble. He looks up at his two teammates. "Guys, could you get me out of here, please?"

Lance scans the opening. It's wide enough for two people to have fallen through. The walls consist of loosely packed dirt and man-made debris. "Anything down there with you? How big is it?" Lance calls down. "Is it deep enough to be safe from the storm?"

Oversight shakes his head then yells back up the shaft, "Nope. Sorry. Just dirt and junk. What you see is all there is."

Lance calls down. "Too bad. I was hoping we could ride out the storm here instead of trying to locate the shelter."

"Can you get me out?" Deforest's voice comes back up to the two on the rim.

"Give us a moment. We need to figure out how to do that without causing the walls to collapse on you." Lance uncoils a loop of rope from his pack. His movement causes loose rubble to bounce down onto Oversight.

"Thanks. Buried alive is not how I'd like to go."

"We'll see what we can do about that," the large gunner chuckles.

Lance glances around but sees no place to anchor the rope. "I guess we're going to have to do it the hard way. Boomslang..." Viper tosses the end of the rope to the gunner, who attaches the end to his waist. "Are you okay with this? How's the arm?"

Kingston grunts a reply, then says, "Don't worry about me. I can always be dead weight." He chuckles, but Lance gets the impression his gunner is making an effort. Lance loops the line around his own waist and then his belt to act as a strain relief. With both men flat on their stomachs, Lance tosses the free end of the rope down into the shaft. The light from his lamp reflects the white of the line that looks like a squiggling snake as it falls toward Oversight.

Deforest reaches up but the rope is beyond his reach. He leaps and strains to grab the end of the rope. He lands hard, misses the rope, and causes the loose walls of his prison to cascade around his legs. "Shit!" he curses. Deforest freezes in place, afraid to cause a further collapse. Lance echoes the curse. If Kingston curses, it is to himself. Deforest looks down in the dim light at the rubble piled up around his ankles. He calls up, "I guess I won't try that again. Guys! I can't reach the rope. Have any other ideas?"

Lance looks over at Kingston beside him. "Let's tie your rope onto this one." Lance reels the rope back up to the surface.

"No can do. Remember? We used it to climb down that ravine."

Lance curses silently. He had forgotten. They had to abandon the rope because the hold fast failed to release and they had never asked for a replacement in a drop. His mind races to come up with an alternate plan. "Okay, forget that." He unsecures the loops around his waist. "This should provide enough slack. Boomslang, you'll have to carry most of the weight. I'll help as much as I can. Are you up to it?"

Kingston forces a grin at Viper. "Sure. No problem. He's a lightweight."

Lance calls down into the hole. "Here it comes again. You should be able to reach it." He tosses the rope down into the shaft.

Deforest reaches for the rope and grabs the end. "Got it! You guys ready?"

Lance glances at Kingston, who nods. He then calls over the edge as he grasps the rope between his hands, "All set. Come on up!"

The slack in the rope disappears and Lance grunts as Deforest's weight tries to pull Kingston and him toward the hole. Deforest pulls himself out of the debris with his hands and then once he is high enough along the rope he braces himself with his feet. He hangs a moment, making sure the rope and his grip on it are firm. Then he pulls himself up the rope hand over hand. The rope chafes against the rim of the opening, releasing a cloud of dirt, dust, and debris onto Deforest's head. He sneezes but continues climbing. The earth under the rope tumbles down in ever-increasing amounts until the weak walls give way and crumble and collapse, dropping Deforest into the hole covering him. Deforest's muffled yell is cut off as the debris buries him.

"Fuck!" Lance springs to his feet and grabs the rifle at his back. He jumps onto the hill of debris, which now sits a meter below the surface. He furiously digs at the debris with the butt of the weapon. Boomslang shovels material away from the hole with his uninjured hand and arm. The men work at a fevered pace until the cascade is cleared enough to expose Oversight's head. Deforest is unconscious, his head and face covered in dust and dirt.

"Is he alive?" Boomslang's voice is quiet with concern.

Viper stoops beside the buried man and places two fingers along his neck. "He's alive. Let's get him out and check him for injuries."

Several frantic minutes of digging later they have Deforest lying on solid ground. Their comms member breathes but is unconscious. Lance pulls his plastic water bottle out of his pack and pours it into Oversight's mouth. The man's eyes flutter open and he struggles to sit up, coughing. Lance presses him back down with a hand. "Lie still."

Deforest stops fighting and relaxes on the ground. "What happened?"

"The shaft collapsed as you were coming up. You were buried and without air for a minute or so. We still don't know if you've broken anything. How do you feel?"

His grin is weak. "Like a ton of rocks fell on me." In a more serious tone, he adds, "I'm okay. But I think I swallowed a bunch of dirt."

"He's okay. I couldn't find anything broken," Boomslang announces as he finishes examining his teammate's arms and legs. "He'll probably ache and have a few bruises for a while." Boomslang reaches into Oversight's bag and pulls out a pain pill from the med pack. The gunner breaks the capsule against Oversight's exposed shoulder. "That should help."

"You up to traveling?" Lance asks Deforest.

"Yeah. Not like I have a choice with the storm, but yeah."

Lance extends a hand and helps the man to his feet. "Are you sure? We can wait another minute if you want."

"No. I'm fine, thanks." Oversight takes a step and pauses. "Give me a few seconds. I'm still tasting dirt." He reaches back and pull his water bottle out. He takes a swig, swishes it around, and spits it out.

The gunner asks, "Better?"

"Yeah. Let's go. I don't want to drag you guys down."

Lance says, "I'll let you rest and recover later. We need to get a move on." Lance checks his watch and direction then sets off toward shelter. Oversight follows and Boomslang brings up the rear. A few steps later, Oversight speaks. "Oh, and thanks for digging me out. I owe you."

Viper glances back over his shoulder. "No problem. We're a team. I need to make sure you guys stay safe until we're decommissioned. After that, it's all up to you. Besides, it's not like we can get a replacement comms while the sats are down." Lance grins at Deforest then resumes the pace.

Boomslang slaps Deforest's shoulder. "Yeah, we're a team. It's not like we'd leave one of us behind."

Lance walks in the front, cursing himself for letting the accident happen.

CHAPTER 30 - LANCE

Lance leads the way. As he walks he relives the moments up to the accident. He'd been sloppy. He should have guessed the mountain of debris wasn't stable. They'd been lucky they were able to dig Deforest out in time. The outcome could have been a lot worse. His mission was to keep the team alive, to get them home. He promises himself he'll do better.

"How much further?" Kingston asks a minute of walking later.

Lance scans the area. "Why? You getting tired, big guy?" He shakes off his own fatigue.

"Nah. I just don't like the looks of the sky."

Lance glances skyward. "Yeah. I don't either." He points at a hill several hundred yards away. "It should be on that hill, I'd say. It's the only one that looks like it might have been something in the past. How are you holding up, Deforest? Any problems?"

"Just a bit sore and I could use a scrubbing, but nothing to complain about."

"Good. We're almost there, team. Just a bit further and we're home free." Lance glances into Kingston's yellow eyes and sees pain and tiredness. Lance then scrambles down the gentle slope in from of them to the large flat plain that stretches to the hill.

"I wonder what this place used to be," the gunner asks. "Look at the ground. It's mostly concrete."

"Yeah. It doesn't look like it's in bad shape. Just a few cracks here and there." Deforest points at a crack filled with struggling weeds.

"Whatever it was, it was big." Lance stops halfway to their target and scans the flat expanse. Something nags at him beyond his hair standing on end due to the coming storm. "Stay sharp. There's no cover here if we're attacked. Let's hustle to that hill. There's at least enough junk there to hide behind. I don't like being this exposed."

"What are you afraid of?" Boomslang asks from behind. "It's not like nasties use guns."

"Yeah, but they can see us coming and we probably won't see them until it's too late. I get the feeling someone's watching us. Move!" Viper sprints through the humid air toward the distant hill. Boomslang and Oversight keep pace. They cover the distance to the base of the hill without incident, then stop to catch their breath.

Viper's instincts scream at him. Something is watching them. He scans the rise in front of them but sees nothing. "Let's find that entrance and get under cover." His nerves are on edge as the dread in him grows.

CHAPTER 31 - RYKER

Ryker walks up the slope to where he had spotted the object when the firefight had broken out. He isn't sure of the exact location since the gunfire had caused him to scuttle away, but he's certain he can find the round metal thing again. A minute later he stands over a grate. He kneels and examines it closely. Strangely it shows no signs of rust or decay. There's dirt, but the object looks as if it was made yesterday. Or so he thinks, since he has no clue what it is. He wraps his claws around the bars and pulls. The object refuses to budge, so he redoubles his efforts with the same effect. Panting, he gives up struggling after a few more moments and peers at the mysterious object. On closer inspection he spots two clasps along one half of the object and hinges on the other. It takes a few moments of fumbling before he figures out the mechanism.

The clasps flip away and he pulls the grate one more time. This time the object swings open, revealing the darkness below. The rungs of a metal ladder disappear beyond the limits of his sight. Ryker stands and scans the area, making sure there are no humans and no packs that might contest his find. Satisfied, he grasps the sides of the opening and lowers his legs onto the ladder. His mutated, elongated body makes it awkward, but he manages to descend rung by rung down into the darkness. He pauses to let his eyes adjust and looks around as he clings to the ladder. He sees the circle of clouded sky above and can just about make out his hands and the rung it grasps. Everywhere else is black, a black he has never known. A shiver runs through him and he considers scurrying up the ladder to light and safety, but the lure of what is below and shelter overwhelm his desire to escape. Taking a deep breath and trying to steady his nerves, he lowers himself carefully, rung by rung.

Minutes later the circle of safety above has become a pinpoint of light that beckons him, calls to him, the way his mother had. He misses her.

His memory of her is vague. It is clouded and probably mutated the way he had been. He holds his hand to the bag that contains his locket, conjuring an image of her in his mind. He long ago stopped wishing to regain his humanity, but he never stops wishing he had had more time with his mother.

He takes several deep breaths and glances down at the vanta-black below him. He wonders for an instant how far it goes. He wonders for several long seconds about what treasures it held, then he continues downward into the unknown.

Half an hour later the sky is gone as the claws on his foot click as they hit the surface below him. Ryker's heart races as he stands. His head swivels from side to side, anticipating surprise or attack from the Stygian expanse around him. He takes a step into the blackness, his heart pounding.

CHAPTER 32 - LANCE

Lance glances over at Kingston, who is struggling to keep up. "You okay?" he asks. Kingston blinks and Lance sees his teammate's effort to focus on him.

"I—I'm fine. Don't worry about me."

"You're not fine." Lance moves to Kingston's side and rips the bandage off the wound. Kingston flinches. Even though it has been sterilized and sealed, the wound looks raw and milky. Lance holds a hand out to Deforest, who hands over the med kit. Lance pulls out a roll of gauze, then pours a liquid on it. "This may hurt a bit. Your wound's infected." Boomslang nods and Lance wipes the wound clean. Kingston grits his teeth but says nothing. Lance pulls a spray canister out of the kit and applies a sealant coat to the wound. He then wraps it in a new bandage. "That should hold you for a while."

The pain had focused Kingston. He grimaces then says, "Thanks, Boss." He moves his arm to the rifle on his other arm but the effort elicits a groan. His arm drops down to his side.

"You've got an infection. You should be okay for now. I still need to get you to meds. I don't like the look of the wound." Lance repacks the kit and hands it back to Oversight.

"You'll be killing nasties in no time," Deforest encourages.

Lance grimaces but doesn't respond. The wound of the gunner is deep and a chunk of bone is gone. The infection is cleaned, but he had seen the milky oozing resurface as he had applied the bandage. He curses to himself, vowing to make things right. "Let's get going. We still need to get to shelter." *I need to get Kingston to real help*, he thinks.

CHAPTER 33 - LANCE

"Okay, this should be it. Look for anything that might be an entrance," Viper commands. "You two stay together and stay alert and in sight. I don't want to take any chances. We don't have time to waste." He glances up at the sky, nervous. Boomslang stays close to Oversight and the men start going through the debris at the top of the hill that had been their goal. Lance pushes aside the loose dirt and the various bits of concrete, plastic, and metal that at one point had been a complex of some sort. He picks up a rusted metal sign too faded and deteriorated to read. Flinging it aside, he watches it spin through the air and land with a clang a dozen yards away. A bit of plastic peeks out of the debris and catches his attention. He stoops down and clears the item of dirt. It's a small plastic box. Using his thumb, Lance flips the lid open. Apart from a thick film of dust, the only thing the box contains is a small hunk of tarnished metal. Lance can make out the faint outline of an eagle and the number 2021. He tosses the worthless coin back into the box, which he then throws away.

He continues scraping at the ground with his boot and rifle butt as he searches for the entrance to the shelter. The hairs on the back of his neck stand on end and tingle. They have been a constant reminder the storm is nearing. He glances up to make sure his team is okay. "Anything?" he calls out.

"Nothing yet," Oversight yells back.

"Just dirt and useless junk, as always. Are you sure we're at the right spot?" Boomslang asks as he trudges back toward Viper.

Viper pulls a map out of his pouch. "Without sat help I can't be certain, but this should be the hill."

"I've got something!" Oversight is on his knees and digging with his hands. Boomslang and Viper jog over to Oversight.

"Is it the entrance?" Boomslang asks as he peers down at the square metal plate Kingston has exposed.

"I don't know, but this is the only thing I've found that might be."

"Can you get it open?" Viper asks, seeing there's no handle.

Oversight runs a finger around the edge of the plate. "There's a rim underneath. I don't feel a latch or anything that could be a handle. We could try prying it up, I guess."

"It's worth a shot, but I would think an entrance would have some sort of mechanism to open it." Viper stoops and draws the knife from his belt. He slips the blade under the plate and runs it around the rim. "Nothing. I don't want to break the blade of my knife. Let's find something we can use to lever it up if we can."

A few moments later they find a long strip of metal that isn't corroded that they jam under the plate. Lance grabs the end of the lever and presses down with all of his weight. "It shifted!" Oversight exclaims. "Try it again." Grunting, Lance throws his entire body weight onto the lever. The plate shifts, the dirt around it loosens, and the square of metal goes flying end over end. Viper slams into the ground, cursing. He picks himself up, brushes himself off, and joins Boomslang and Oversight by the hole.

The three peer down. "Well, that was a waste of time," Oversight mumbles.

"Yup," Viper agrees.

Boomslang curses as he stares down at the dirt that was under the metal plate. "We're lost, aren't we? We have no idea where the entrance is and the storm is almost on us." He points to the sky.

Viper sighs, then drops to sit on the ground. He pulls the map out again. He asks, "Kingston, give me those coordinates again," but thinks, *Hell, why did the sats have to die?* Oversight stoops beside Viper, flips his visor down, and reads the coordinates of the shelter. The visor goes back up. "Yeah. That's what I had. Without the sats, the best I can do is track our time and direction walked. This should be the place."

"Maybe the sats were wrong," Boomslang suggests. "They were acting up before they went silent."

Oversight thinks a moment. "Maybe. I guess it's possible they sent garbage, but I think I got the coords before things began to get flaky."

"So what do we do now?" Boomslang's voice quavers and is weak.

Lance glances at one then the other of his team before he answers. "The entrance must be here. Spread out. Find it." Lance doesn't add that if they don't, they don't have the time to find something else. All of them know their survival depends on finding the shelter.

CHAPTER 34 - LANCE

Lance moves away from the others and searches the area toward the edges of the flattened hill. The fact that it is flat tells him they are near. He takes several steps, scrapes away at the surface, and, not finding the entrance, repeats the process as he goes. Every so often he checks in with his teammates. His nerves on edge, he glances around frequently. He's uncomfortable being out of sight, but he knows this is the fastest way to cover the most ground. He glances up at a sky that's darker than he's ever seen—and greener. It seems to press down on him and his mood. The brim of his cap is darker than he's ever seen it as well. He could die on this hill if they didn't find the shelter—they all could. He had, of course, thought about death. The possibility an accident or, more likely, a scavenger would kill him was part of the job. He had never dwelt on the possibility but now he is spending more time than usual contemplating his own death. The more he thinks about it, the more depressed he gets. He can't see past his own nonexistence. The blackness in his soul grows.

Shaking himself of the foul mood, Lance redoubles his effort to find the shelter. His mind keeps snapping him back, however. He curses and focuses on the mission at hand. Viper has to keep his team safe—alive. The dull glow of the sun behind the ill clouds casts long shadows. It will be night soon. Viper's mind races to find an alternate solution to the problem of shelter, but none come to mind apart from digging the team in and hoping they will survive. Rad storms have penetrated most of the materials that cover the surface now. The only certain safety is being deep enough under it where the radiation can't penetrate. He glances at his watch. Viper doubts they can dig deep enough in the time they had left. But digging is all he has. He presses the bud to call his team back and order them to dig in when Boomslang's voice interrupts him.

"I think I got it."

A minute later the three stand over a large plate of metal. It's corroded, but the writing is dimly legible around large rusted holes. "C. 20mi. E. Ft. — North Entrance 20mi."

"I don't get it." Deforest stares down at the ancient sign.

Lance curses. "The North Entrance is twenty miles from here. We're on the wrong hill."

"Twenty miles? But in which direction?" Boomslang asks.

"East." The tone of Oversight's voice tells Lance frustration is setting in.

"We have some running to do." Viper waves the group east.

"It feels like we've been walking forever. Now we have to run?"

"Only if you want to stay alive. Run!" Desperate to outrace the storm, Lance dashes toward their goal.

CHAPTER 35 - RYKER

Ryker sees nothing. His heart beats into his throat and is the only comforting sound in the darkness. He stands by the bottom rungs, looking around, anticipating, worried of threats unseen. None come. He waits for what feels like an eternity, but there's only silence as dark as the black around him. His only reality is the wall his hand presses as an anchor. He pants, his nerves on edge. There's not enough air here, or so he feels. Ryker glances up the ladder and sees darkness. He wants to escape but can't see the light he had left. He isn't sure it's even there. His clawed hand goes to his bag and pulls out the small locket. He looks down at it and is uncertain it's there—the darkness is complete. He puts his valuable back, careful not to drop it into the darkness that surrounds him.

He still has his memories. His mind pictures his mother, her hair, her smile. She died in the blast. She died in her sleep, never waking to the horror the world had become. The thought is comforting in a macabre sort of way. Humans took her away. Humans took his humanity away, but he is still human. He steps into the darkness. *Humans have to pay.*

CHAPTER 36 - LANCE

"Is this it?" Oversight glances down at a grate that opens to a dark shaft.

"It must be." Viper can't imagine anything else that would be deep enough to provide shelter from the storm. "Without comms I can't be certain, but this looks deep enough to be safe."

"I don't like it." Boomslang peers down into the darkness. "It's deep. What if we're trapped down there? I—I don't like enclosed spaces."

"We'll be fine. It's either that or stay out here and be fried by the rad winds." Lance hops down onto a rung and looks up at his teammates. "Just stay sharp and have your lanterns on." To accentuate his point, he flicks on the torch built into his hat. "Don't let your guard down. It doesn't look like anything has breached this entrance, but that's no reason to get sloppy." He starts the long descent into the darkness. Deforest and Kingston follow.

The team makes steady progress down the shaft. But because of Boomslang's injury and dizziness, their progress is slow. A half hour later all three stand at the bottom, the beams from their hats sweeping the small chamber in which they find themselves.

"What is this place?" Kingston asks, pointing at a sealed door on one side of the room.

"It looks like an old missile silo. I guess the aboveground bunker is long gone." Lance sets out toward the door, kicking up the undisturbed dust that sparkles in the beams coming from their hats.

"I hope there is food." Boomslang's voice is tired and spent.

"I doubt anything left over from then is something you'd want to eat." Lance shoots a grin at his teammate. *At least,* he thinks, *we made it to safety.* Now they just have to wait out the storm. "Deforest, any idea how long the storm will last?"

The young man shakes his head. "Without comms I have no way to say when it will hit or how long it will be until it's safe to pull out. My best guess is we should probably sit tight a full week given the storm's intensity."

Lance pulls on the door but it refuses to budge. He examines the ancient key card slot a moment, pulls up his rifle, and shoots a bullet into the long-dead mechanism, shattering it into a shower of metal and plastic shards. He pulls a spare battery out of his backpack and connects two of the now-exposed wires. He's rewarded with a loud click as the door's latch disengages.

"Where did you learn that trick?" Deforest asks, impressed.

Lance shrugs, grinning. "I had a misspent youth studying ancient motor vehicles. They were a lot simpler than the ones now despite the interfaces." He pushes the door open and steps through. Oversight and Boomslang follow, their lamps illuminating shafts of dust. Lance feels his skin on the back of his neck prickle to attention.

CHAPTER 37 - RYKER

There is nothing but the black and Ryker hears nothing but his own heartbeat and breathing. He's breathing fast. He doesn't like being blind. His hands and claws stretch in front of him, moving at random, seeking as he takes hesitant steps forward. What he searches for he doesn't know. A few moments later he freezes, his mind racing in fear. *What if I get lost? What if I can't find the ladder again?* In a panic, he retraces his steps then breathes a sigh of relief when he bumps into the metal ladder. He stands until his tension subsides to a manageable level. For a moment he considers escaping this pit, climbing to the unseen light, and running home. Then he remembers the prickling of his skin, which has subsided, and the approaching storm. He will be safe here, no matter the strength of the storm. He will wait it out. After all, the opening has been barred. He is alone here. He moves forward again, feeling ahead as he does so. Despite his self-assurance the fear and trepidation grow. He hisses and flinches back as his claws scrape an unseen wall. When no attack comes, he forces his breathing and nerves to calm. His hand reaches out and the wall is still there. It's metal. He feels the smooth surface with the pads of his fingers feeling the coolness. Then it hits him—the air here is cool, chilly in fact. He'd forgotten how it could be. The world above is humid and hot. Here, below ground, it is humid but the heat is shielded by rock and stone. His breath comes easier and he has more energy. His fear and stress had blinded him to the change. Ryker feels good. Ryker feels strong. Still, the darkness holds unknown terrors.

He resumes his search, tapping along the wall. Several minutes later he stumbles on a door. Ryker probes around its periphery and finds a panel and latch. An instant later he discovers the door isn't sealed. There's a gap along one side of the door where the metal is bent and deformed, the result of shifts in the ground. Earthquakes had become more common since the war and Ryker guesses the seal had broken during one such event. He grasps the door and shoves, but the metal slab refuses to budge. Taking several deep breaths, he summons his strength and yanks on the free edge of the door. The metal complains with a loud screech that echoes up the shaft behind him, but it yields to his pull and bends inward.

Ryker can't see the results of his effort, but he can feel the opening is large enough that he can pass. He slides sideways through the door, but freezes as ancient lights flicker to life around him, momentarily blinding him as they do. He cowers by the door, unsure what has occurred.

CHAPTER 38 - LANCE

"So, this is an old-timey missile silo, huh?" Kingston points at the faded metal sign by a massive door that is half open. His voice is tired and his face pale. The gunner catches Lance examining him. He throws a weak grin at Viper. "Don't worry. I'll make it. Just need to get some rest when we get a chance." Lance nods and moves through the opening.

"Look at all this old tech!" Oversight whistles in awe as his hat lantern swings through the dark room. "I saw things like this in a museum as a kid." He walks over to a panel and runs a finger through the layer of thick dust. "I'm surprised it hasn't decayed or been scavenged."

"Constant temperature down here. They built these to withstand a nuke blast," Viper explains, pulling open an old locker. It's empty. "Scavengers probably don't know about it. We had Gov to tell us when the sats were still up." He examines a small tarnished plaque on the metal wall.

"This is the kind of place that ended the Gaman war. Crazy bastards gave us the world we live in." Kingston pauses in thought. "You don't suppose the missile is still here, do you?"

Lance walks toward the center of the room. His light crosses paths with Boomslang's. He shakes his head, his beam dancing across the far wall. "Doubt it. What wasn't launched on Old Philly probably got scrapped for resources once the country's economy tanked. I remember reading about the food riots and trade wars after the East Coast went under. They needed every bit of tech and metal they could hold onto. Once the rest of the world declared the old country off-limits there would've been no reason to keep the nukes that were still around. The country had become a pariah. What missiles were left were scrapped, the leaders of the time fearing destroying more of the world."

A small green light springs to life on one of the consoles in front of Deforest. Its blinking casts and eerie glow over the room and its three inhabitants. "What the hell did you do? Don't touch anything!" Viper quickly moves to Deforest's side, staring at the tiny bulb.

"I–I didn't do anything. I was just standing here looking at the layout when it suddenly came on!"

As they watch the panel flickers and a Christmas tree selection of colored lights illuminates the panel. An instant later long-dark overhead lamps burst into light, causing the three to swivel in place, their guns springing to ready positions. The three are instantly back to back. Kingston clutches a pistol in his good hand. A low humming whir fills the room. "What the hell?" The team's eyes flick from place to place, seeking out the threat, their fingers on the triggers of their weapons.

"Stand easy but stay alert. We triggered some sort of system—maybe our body heat or movement." Lance takes one last scan of the room, relaxes his grip on his rifle, and exhales a long breath. Boomslang and Oversight are still frozen in place, their caution still evident. A moment later first one then the other relaxes.

"This place gives me the creeps," Boomslang spits at one of the consoles. "It's like it's alive and we're in it."

"At least we're safe from the storm." Lance glances at his watch. "It's over us right now." He sniffs the air. "The old recirculators must have kicked in. It's not as musty as it was when we came in. Make yourselves at home. We have to wait at least a week to make sure the storm has passed. We're going to be here a while." He takes a moment to survey the now-lit room. It's rectangular with the bank of consoles along one metal wall and a large metal table or desk in the middle of the room. The skeletons of three metal chairs are scattered about, their cushions and padding having disintegrated long ago. Lance pulls one of the chairs upright, sits down on the metal webbing that forms the seat, then pulls his rations out of his pack along with the photo of Roxy. He stares at it as he chews the dry food pack. He wonders what she is doing, whether she is eating and what. He wonders if she misses him the way he misses her. For a moment he second-guesses his decision to not allow her to sign up with him, then realizes for the hundredth time that there was no guarantee she would have been shipped with his team. It is better this way. At least she is safe at home.

As he eats, Lance glances at the blinking console lights. He'd learned about the old tech as had everyone. He envies their ability to send messages and even images as easily as speaking. But the war had destroyed all that. The only tech belongs to Gov, and even that is degrading day by day the way the sats had. Lance glances over at Kingston. The large man sits on the floor in a corner of the room, eating his ration. His face is paler than it has ever been. Lance curses, looking away when the gunner notices his stare. Deforest is examining the panels, but plays it safe by keeping his hands behind his back.

Lance repacks the remainder of his rations and carefully replaces the photo of Roxy. He touches a finger to his lips and then the pack that contains his love. He pushes himself off the uncomfortable chair and walks over to his gunner. "Time to redress your wound." He kneels and motions to Oversight, who tosses him the med pack. Lance rips the old dressing off and winces. The wound is milky with tinges of green. The sanitizer hasn't taken. The wound is infected and not clearing. He cleans and bandages Kingston's arm. He then pulls an ampule out of the kit and slams one end of it into the gunner's shoulder. Boomslang winces but says nothing, which is unusual for the large man. *The antibiotics should do what the sterilizer hasn't*, Lance thinks. He then gives Kingston's hand a quick pat, packs up the med kit, and walks it over to Deforest.

His comms man glances up and takes the pack from Lance. "I can make out most of this stuff but I don't get these two displays." He points at one with a single number on it in green characters. It reads '4.' It doesn't have a label under it like most of the others, so I have no idea what it means."

Lance glances at the display. "Maybe that's how many silos there are."

"No, that's over here." Oversight points at another plastic rectangle. "And get this." For emphasis he carefully wipes the dust from the display with a finger. "It says there is one nuke in the tube—the other four are empty."

Lance's eyebrows shoot up. "We have a nuke? Is it live? Maybe the four is the number missing."

"Hard to say if it's live or not, but there's something in the tube the system thinks is a missile."

"We need to find out if it is and get the intel to Gov. He didn't say anything about a nuke being here, did he?"

Oversight shakes his head. "When I asked for safe haven from the storm he pointed us here but didn't say anything about it having a nuke. He would have alerted us if he had known. My guess is he found the site in old data and figured it had been scrubbed years ago."

A moan escapes from Kingston, drawing Lance's and Deforest's attention away from the console. Lance looks from his gunner to his comms guy. "He's in bad shape. He's got an infection sterilization didn't get. I gave him antibios, but those will take time."

Deforest looks over at his teammate. There are beads of sweat evident on the gunner's face. "He needs a full-body cleanse."

"You don't have one in your bag of tricks, do you?"

Oversight grimaces. "Not likely." He pauses in thought. "They must've had a med facility at these nuke sites."

"They didn't have cleanses back then—but I get where you're going. Maybe they had something that would help." Lance adjusts the rifle on his back. "If it's still viable."

Oversight shrugs. "It's the best I can do unless we can get him to a real med center."

"It will have to do. It's not like we have a choice." Lance walks over to Kingston. "Up, big guy. Time to move out." The gunner glances up with red eyes but manages to stand on his own. "Priority number one," Viper continues, "find the med center. Priority two, find out if we really have a nuke." Lance looks around the chamber and wonders why he doesn't feel as safe as he should.

CHAPTER 39 - RYKER

Ryker straightens, exhaling deeply once he senses no nearby threat. He surveys the large room as his eyes adjust to the artificial light. It's a circular room with old metal catwalks whose white paint has long flaked off. The roof is hidden beyond the reach of the lights that encircle the room at floor level. He ignores all of that but instead stands and stares at the object in the center of the room. It is large, very tall, cylindrical, and pointed at the top. There are fins along its side. His mind struggles to take in the sight until ancient memories of war spark recognition. A missile. His head swivels in all directions, searching for the humans. Where there are missiles there are bound to be humans. His heart beats a staccato against his chest. A minute later he relaxes. There is no one here. He is alone. His gaze returns to the object of fear and dread, not only for him and his kind, but for all of humanity. He takes a tentative step forward as ancient terrors and memories flood over him. He flinches involuntarily. His face breaks out into a sweat, the only part of him still capable of sweating. His body armor will be of little use if the missile goes off, and his head is still vulnerable to rads. Nature had cursed him when it had spared him and made him stronger, but it had cursed him by leaving his head and face as fragile as it had been before the war. Nature had extended his life over hundreds of years, but at the same time that meant he had more memories and life to lose. Humans had done this to him and no longer considered him human, humans long dead because they had not changed. But his memory was long.

No explosion. No rads—his skin didn't tingle. He takes careful steps toward the metal cylinder. Oblivion does not come even as he fearfully touches a claw to the thing. He grows bolder and places the palm of his hand on it, feeling the ancient dust and its uncaring coolness. He peers up the shaft toward the tip but can't see it. This was once a weapon of war—they had defeated the Gamans but the war had ripped the world and his country apart. It had cost him his humanness.

The metal under his palm is cold, unfeeling, uncaring. Ryker stands in silence and in a sense of almost communion with the object that had destroyed him and his world. Then in the silence a plan forms. He's uncertain if it's his or the device's, but he likes it. He will use this against the humans. He gives one more glance upward then lopes toward the door on the opposite side of the tube and into the next chamber.

CHAPTER 40 - LANCE

"Movement dead ahead." Oversight's rife comes up as he barks the warning.

Lance peers and sees nothing, but his weapon comes up nonetheless. "Are you sure? Maybe it was more systems coming online."

"Sure. It was moving left to right. I couldn't make out what it was."

"Eyes sharp. No sense in taking chances. Boomslang, you up to this?" Viper examines his gunner from toe to head. He's moving slowly, but he's up and focused. The pistol in his good hand isn't as good as a rifle, but it's something. Boomslang nods but his usual gung-ho is not evident. The infection has taken its toll. "SH-2, stay close. I want to keep an eye on you. I don't want you passing out on me—no arguments." He has to keep his team safe and alive. "SH-3, flank right behind the target. Click on sight."

Boomslang winces but doesn't argue as he shuffles beside Viper. Oversight, rifle ready, moves to the right in the direction opposite his target's travel. Viper and Boomslang move as a single unit, crouching as they go in the direction of the movement. Lance glances over at Kingston and is relieved to see his gunner keeping up and alert despite the pallor of his face.

The chamber they're in is large—several hundred yards on either side—and full of metal canisters and the remains of wooden ones that have fallen to dust and piles of indiscernible refuse. Tall metal pillars stand comb-like down the center of the large chamber. The duo moves forward, pausing every few steps to scan the area ahead and behind. Viper's rifle, scope up, is at eye level, ready to fire on sight. Boomslang's pistol is held at waist level; his left hand hangs limply by his side. The hum of the air circulators has Lance on edge. After years of disuse they don't run smoothly and an occasional stutter or clang makes him flinch, expecting the worst. His bud is silent, an indication Oversight hasn't encountered the target. Lance's narrowed focus is on the gunsight and what lies beyond it, but a part of his mind wonders if they are chasing ghosts.

"I hate this place," Boomslang grumbles under his breath, but loudly enough to be heard. Viper shoots him a silencing glance but agrees with him without saying so. The bunker is supposed to be safe, but it's also supposed to be deserted. He wants, needs a break. Ten years waiting, and no decom has come from Gov. Now that the sats are down, his mind wanders and wonders if it ever will.

A click in their buds brings Viper and Boomslang's attention back to the problem at hand. Viper speaks through his teeth. "Nothing here," Boomslang confirms.

"Shit!" Oversight's voice exclaims into their buds.

Lance's senses switch into overdrive. "What's wrong? You okay?"

"Yeah. Fine," Oversight replies, his voice on edge but reassuring. "Biggest scavenger I've ever seen."

Viper's sights swivel, searching for the target. "Nothing here. Sure it's a nasty?"

"Yeah, twice as big and twice as ugly. Must be ten feet head to toe."

"Shit!" Kingston exclaims beside him. "How did it get that big?"

Lance lets the breach of silence go and speaks to the bud. "How many?" A pack of nasties is hard enough to handle without having to deal with oversized ones. There is a pause as Oversight scans the area around the creature in his scope. "One. I see no others, large or small."

"Don't engage. We still need an intact brain."

"You're kidding, right?"

Lance shrugs even though Deforest can't see him. "It's as good a time as any and we have a loner."

"I think I'd prefer to engage a pack than this sucker." The bud in Lance's ear crackles. "How do you want to proceed?"

"We still need to acquire him. Where is he?" Lance wishes the sats were up. They would have helped triangulate the position based on their rifle sights. Now they have to rely on dead sightings.

"He's behind the third pillar in front of me."

"What's he doing?"

"Not sure. He's just standing looking around."

"Stay out of sight."

"You don't have to tell me twice, Boss."

Viper signals to Boomslang and the two creep forward toward the metal post, scanning as they go. Viper's bud crackles back to life. "I have eyes on you. He's ten yards to your right. He's looking up at something." Lance steals a glance upward and spots catwalks. He refocuses his attention on the pillar in front of them. The two men move forward silently and slowly. A long arm, longer than any he'd seen in his time as a hunter, moves to wrap around the metal column. An instant later, the twin of the arm comes in from the other side. Viper clicks the earbud three short taps to indicate they are moving in. Oversight acknowledges with a single click. Lance remains crouching, his scope trained on the target. Lance breaks silence and whispers, "Neck shots only. We need that brain intact." Two clicks come back separated by a second or two. Oversight is set. Boomslang is set.

Lance and the gunner inch their way forward, circling the pillar while keeping their gunsights on the creature in front of them. Oversight had warned them of the creature's size, but Lance still inhales with surprise as he moves into direct line with it. It's taller than a man and taller than any scavenger he'd encountered. It was scrambling up the pillar oblivious to the men hunting it. "Am hot. Have a shot," Oversight's whisper tells Viper.

"Take 'em if you got 'em," Lance whispers back. "Let's get that brain." *Things are looking up*, he thinks.

CHAPTER 41 - RYKER

The chamber Ryker is in is larger than the one with the missile, but the ceiling is visible in the artificial light. Metal pillars spaced at regular intervals in the chamber bring back memories of old-world museums and monuments. He hasn't thought about or even remembered them in years, but a memory of his human life and visiting a museum in the now burned-out Philadelphia makes him pause and touch a claw to the locket he carries. He will avenge her and himself. He will destroy humans with the missile. His eyes dart around the room but don't find what he needs. He has to find the control room and a way to launch the deadly object. The room is littered with canisters and objects that block his view. He glances up and spots the ladder-like catwalks above but sees no way up to them. He stands by a metal pillar, considering his options. He can wander the large chamber, hoping to stumble on the control room, or he can get up high and more easily find the entrance he is seeking. He glances up one last time, then wraps his arms around the pillar closest to him. He begins shimmying up the cold metal, anchoring himself as he rises with the claws of his feet. He clambers upward and is halfway up when a movement below him catches his eye. He twists to make out what it is as a shot rings out.

The impact startles him and he instinctively pulls back and, in so doing, lets go of the pillar. He plummets to the ground, hitting hard on his back. He lays stunned for a second then quickly rolls over, catching his breath. His brain scrambles to make sense of what has happened, but fixes on the two figures approaching him, their weapons drawn. Humans! For a moment he considers standing his ground or attacking, but he hasn't survived by being stupid and reckless. It's bad enough he'd let his guard down and assumed he was alone in this human complex. Panic floods his mind. The two are moving closer. Part of him wonders why they don't fire. Another part of him judges the closing distance between him and his hunters. The panic overrides all thought of escape. Without thinking, he launches himself into the air at the two. Time slows for him. A shot rings out and a bullet whistles past him. The two hadn't fired—they hadn't even reacted to his leap. *There must be others*, he thinks. A hidden human firing is too much to deal with. He has to escape. He sees the look of fear and surprise in the two. One seems to move slowly; his arm hangs limp at his side. The other's rifle comes up and a flash of light followed by the crack of the rifle fire assaults him. The bullets bounce off his chest as he crashes into the one holding the rifle. The human yells something, but Ryker is too hyped on adrenaline to hear. He has to flee while he can—while he has them disoriented while avoiding the shooter he can't see. The human falls under him, trying to roll out of the way. Ryker hisses and takes a wide swipe at the two men. Panicked yells now come from both. The one with the pistol dodges his claw and fires off a shot that goes wide of his head. Ryker doesn't wait for them to recover but turns and sprints across the metal floor, zigzagging between the pillars and various containers strewn about the chamber.

Shouts mix with shots as he scrambles to increase the distance between the humans and himself while at the same time trying to interpose as many obstacles as he can between the bullets and himself. Fear, panic, and an adrenaline cocktail urge him blindly forward. Ryker pushes himself faster, knowing the humans will chase. An open door beckons in front of him. He doesn't know where it leads, but the doorway could be sealed and offer an obstacle to his hunters. Now he just has to make it without being hit in the head. The lone gunman is his main worry. The two he had attacked will recover in a couple of seconds but, for now, they are still trying to regroup.

He screams as a bullet grazes the side of his face. He redoubles his efforts toward the doorway. Through sheer luck he'd made it this far. His heart pounds in his chest. His lungs struggle to provide enough oxygen to his armor-encased muscles. More bullets speed past him, whistling as they do. Several ping off his armor, causing him to swerve. The two humans have recovered enough to aim. It won't take them much more time to get the range and angle to his head despite his up-and-down and side-to-side movement. The human scopes have an uncanny way of finding their target when in the hands of trained hunters—and most hunters are trained. Those that don't aim well don't survive long. Ryker doesn't plan on being their target longer than he has to. With a final leap he flies through the door and rolls to a stop short of a brightly lit console.

Ryker has no time to examine or admire, so he spins and slides the heavy metal door into the opening. It falls into place with a loud, satisfying clunk. He hasn't noticed if the door has a metal handle on the side facing the humans like the one on this side, and he doesn't know how to lock the door. But it is sealed and he knows if it can withstand a nuke blast, it can probably withstand the humans' bullets. Ryker examines the room and grabs one of the ancient chairs, which he jams against the latch. He doesn't know if it will hold or even slow the humans, but in a small way he feels safer. He lets out a long breath and allows his heart and nerves to relax. He quickly scans the room, if for no other reason than to ascertain that there is another way out and that he hasn't trapped himself. The room is the smallest of the ones he'd been in since he had descended. One wall has a console with various displays. With caution, he walks over to the lights, his claws click-clacking on the metal floor.

His mind takes in the console. He has no clue what the displays are individually. But his mind and his mood soar when he realizes what they do in total. This is the control room for the missile complex. His mind shifts from adrenaline to endorphins as he grins. He has found what he has been looking for. Here is a way to launch the missile and to rain vengeance on the humans who had changed him and had cast him out. All he has to do is figure out how to do it. A staccato causes Ryker to jump in renewed panic. The humans have reached the door.

CHAPTER 42 - LANCE

Lance pulls himself off the ground. He'd rolled, clutching his rifle to his chest, away from the nasty. The creature sprints away as Oversight fires several shots but misses. He glances over at Kingston, who is crouching and firing the pistol one-handed with his good, albeit non-gun hand. The large scavenger zigzags between the pillars and objects in the room, making hitting it harder. Viper brings his rifle up to his shoulder and flips the scope into place. He tracks the creature across the chamber, steadying his shaking hand, slowing his breath and heart, and then slowly squeezes off a shot. He curses as the bullet bounces off the creature's back. Boomslang, next to him, yells and fires. At this distance his bullets have little chance of being accurate, and if he is lucky enough to hit, the pistol will do little damage. "Save your ammo!" Lance yells over to Boomslang. He focuses the scope higher on the lower back of the scavenger's head, going for a neck shot. *Gov needs that brain*, he thinks, *and this is the perfect opportunity*. Lance tracks and times the zigzag and leads the creature by a hair. The rifle fires. Lance absorbs the recoil and sees the creature flinch but not stop its escape. He'd scored a glancing hit as the creature had pulled right. Viper lines up another shot, but the scavenger disappears into the control room from which his team had come. A moment later the thick metal door slams shut.

Lance drops his rifle to a ready position and turns to Boomslang. "Let's go. We can still get him." He then keys the bud. "SH-3, group up. He's holed up in the control room."

"Roger. I saw. Sorry for the miss. The target zigged when he should have zagged. We could have used a real sniper."

"Understood. Don't worry about it. Just don't miss next time." Lance doesn't tell Deforest he'd missed his shot as well. Instead, he rushes forward toward the control room, with Kingston lagging by his side. In frustration he fires a burst at the metal door that pings the bullets in random directions.

"Have you ever seen such a big nasty?" Kingston asks as Deforest joins the two.

Lance shakes his head. "No. I've never even heard of one being that big. But it may explain the team we found earlier."

"You think it killed all three of them?" Deforest asks, his voice sober. "I wonder if there are others like him."

"Don't know, but we either have to take him out or, preferably, get his brain. Gov said he wants a brain, and this will be the granddaddy of them all if we can score it." The team stands outside the sealed room, then Lance signals his comrades, who flank either side of the door, weapons at the ready. Lance crouches and grasps the metal door handle. On signal, he yanks the handle down to open the door. It doesn't budge.

Lance curses then orders his team to pull back behind a pillar where they can talk. "Now what?" Deforest leans out beyond the metal column to take a peek at the door.

"We're locked out unless you have some trick up your sleeve I don't know about. We don't have any explosives, and I'm not even sure a nuke could breach that door." Lance's brow furrows. "Can it cause any damage in there?"

Deforest shakes his head. "I doubt it. I don't think it's smart enough to know what that stuff is. Hell, some of that old tech confuses even me. If you mean can it launch the missile? No way. It can punch or smash all the panels and the safeties will keep the nuke from going up."

Viper nods. "It can escape the way we got in, so there is no sense in waiting it out."

"Now what?" Oversight repeats.

Lance stands, his back braced against the pillar, and considers. His priority is to make sure his team stays safe; his mission is to get a scavenger brain. He glances at Kingston, who is wavering where he stands, his eyes half closed and beads of sweat rolling down his face. Lance moves quickly to the gunner's side. "You don't look good. How are you feeling?"

"I feel worse than I look." A weak grin flashes across his face.

"I believe it." Viper turns to Deforest. "New priority. We need to find the med center like we originally planned. We have to get Kingston back to normal—or as normal as he ever is." He winces at his own weak attempt at humor, but the gunner gives him a crooked smile.

"He's more normal now," Deforest jokes, which elicits a groan from the large man. Viper turns back to Boomslang, glad to see the man's spirits are up, but is shocked when the gunner collapses to the hard floor. Lance and Deforest rush to their fallen comrade's side.

Lance lifts the gunner's head and places it on his own lap. "He's burning up. The infection must've really taken hold." He pulls his water bottle from his belt and pours a few drops onto the gunner's lips.

Deforest rips the dressing from Kingston's arm. "Jeez!" Lance looks at the arm. A red rash has spread from the original wound's edge and the milkiness has been replaced by a dark gray scum. A fetid odor rises around the gunner. Deforest pulls his med kit from his back and cleans and redresses the wound. "Neither the steri or the antibios have done any good."

Lance's mouth sets in a grim line as he pours some water into his gunner's mouth. There is no response. He glances at his watch. The storm is half an hour in now and will still be overhead for several more days at least. There's no way the sats will come up, and the only chance Kingston has is the med center. Lance stands, dragging Boomslang up with him. Viper comes to a decision. "Let's go find that med center. We're not leaving Boomslang behind."

CHAPTER 43 - RYKER

Ryker relaxes once the rattle of bullets against the steel door subsides and no humans come bursting through. The door will hold; he's now sure of it. He hadn't been certain before but the extended silence and no further attempts to break in are promising. Ryker isn't stupid enough to think the humans might not be planning something. He has centuries of experience and knowledge of the humans 'cleverness. His nerves are on edge and he doesn't dare let himself be lulled by the quiet or a false sense of security. Still, he turns his attention to the colorful lights and panels that he's certain are the key to his vengeance.

His memory is long, especially when it comes to what they had done to him and his family, but Ryker's practice of that knowledge has faded with time. He stares at the lettered labels and displays, trying to recall the long-dead meaning. Familiarity does not bring recognition or knowledge. He tries to will himself to remember, but the side of his face still burns and stings from the bullet. A hand goes up and comes away with blood. He curses, but blames himself for the carelessness that had almost cost him his life. Stupidity could undo years of caution and survival. He feels the wound with his finger, careful not to gouge or even touch it with his claw. He'd done that early in the transformation, trying to relieve an itch while he slept, and had awoken with a bloody pillow. That was while he was still human enough to use pillows. The new wound is superficial and will heal, adding another scar to his face. It is not serious enough to be worrisome, but serious enough as a lesson to learn and remember.

Ryker looks down at the displays and one particular display catches his eyes. *Four*, his mind thinks. The recognition makes his heart beat faster. *That's the number four. Four!* He blinks in surprise. *Four what? Four missiles?* He's only seen the one. He scans the room and consoles, looking for the four. There were three chairs, but the ancient humans wouldn't have a display for counting normal things, would they? There are the three humans and himself. That makes four. But why is that important? He has no answer. He stares at the writing, trying to recall its meaning. *I—that's an I.* He finds other i's. He looks at the switches and buttons, willing them to tell him what they did. They remain silent. He's growing tired and hungry. He's had no rest and little food since the previous day. He knows food will have to wait until he finds another way out, but that will have to wait until the storm passes. He can rest now as long as the door holds. Ryker glances at the metal rectangle. There have been no sounds, no attempts at entry. Exhausted, he moves to the center of the room and sinks down onto the floor, facing the door.

CHAPTER 44 - LANCE

"Give me a hand. I'll carry him," Lance says. Deforest helps drape the unconscious man across Lance's shoulders. Lance holds an arm in one hand and a leg in the other, balancing the heavy weight across his own back. He has second thoughts, but this way they won't have to leave Boomslang behind or split up. Also this leaves Oversight free to cover if the need to fire arises. Finally, if he gets too tired, he can transfer the burden to Deforest. He doesn't like this plan, but Lance can't come up with anything better. The sooner they can get Kingston patched up, the better all of them will be. His team is now one man down, two if he includes himself as the carry.

The team moves slowly, Oversight scanning the area as they go, casting cautious glances at the sealed door behind them. A few moments later they come across the entrance that opens to the missile, which towers over them as they pass through the doorway. Oversight whistles in awe, forgetting to protect the team until Viper chastises him. "Stay sharp! Somehow I don't think there are more of those creatures around, but I don't want to make the same mistake twice." Still, Lance takes a moment to stare up at the metal cylinder they are in and the deadly object it houses. Lance's nerves are ragged as he scans the walkway far above. He adjusts Boomslang's weight across his shoulders and moves forward to the only other entrance. Oversight stays close and alert. Several moments later they stand in a small dark chamber with a ladder leading upward. Oversight flicks on the beam on his hat and peers upward into the darkness.

"I'd guess this goes to the surface. It's probably how the big nasty got in without him passing us."

Lance thinks a long moment then says, "We need to backtrack to the other door. They wouldn't have built a med center off of the missile. I should have figured that out before we wasted time looking here." He has to get help to Boomslang and he's wasted time he shouldn't have. If he loses the gunner he won't know what to do to. He's made too many stupid mistakes lately. His mission will fail horribly if he continues the way he has.

He carries the limp body of Kingston back the way they had come into the storage area. The door on the far side that the creature had run through is out of sight, but Lance peers ahead and up the columns, expecting to find the creature up on the walkways. Lance's eyes continue to sweep the room. He is ready to shout and make a break for cover at an instant's notice. They move quickly to the remaining door. This, like the other, is sealed, but opens easily when Oversight pulls the handle. The two men step into the room. The lights flicker on as they do and a moment later Deforest declares the room secure. This room is larger than the control room but smaller than the storage area. The remains of several metal bunks line one wall, metal lockers another.

Anyone who had used this room has long disappeared in the annals of time. Any mementos or objects they may have left have deteriorated to dust, and the dust has itself deteriorated to new dust. Lance chooses the leftmost of the two doors that line a side wall. He flings it open to discover an ancient bathroom. The porcelain is cracked and he doesn't try the taps, which have corroded and no longer exist. He pulls the remaining door open and faces a narrow passageway whose lights flicker to life as he moves into it. "This way," he calls to Oversight, who is examining the remains of the toilet, his rifle still at the ready.

Lance leads the way, even though he knows it would have been more prudent had Oversight led. The gunner's dead weight is wearing on him and his lack of movement makes the search for medical help more urgent. There's a door on either side of the long corridor and one between the two at its end. The med center, if there is one, has to be beyond one of those doors. He moves forward toward the central one as the lights go out.

He stops short, but Kingston, who is covering the rear, isn't quite as quick and runs into him, almost pushing the overburdened leader to the ground. Lance fights to keep his balance in the pitch black while holding on to Boomslang. "Watch it," Viper growls.

Oversight curses behind him then quickly apologizes. The comm's lantern flares into light, shooting its beam into the leader's eyes, blinding him. Deforest apologizes again, swiveling his lamp down toward the floor. Lance is about to lash out but holds back, realizing it was accidental and the loss of power caught both of them unprepared. "Why'd the power go out?" Deforest asks, his voice tinged with fear and worry. His lamp swivels up and down the corridor but he makes certain it doesn't cross Lance's eyes again.

"Who knows why they came on? We should count ourselves lucky we had light and air for as long as we did given the age of this complex." The air would become stale now that the recirculators had lost power. "Let's keep going. We still need to fix up Boomslang. Stay on your toes. We don't want to be ambushed in the dark. Speaking of which, turn my lantern on, will you? My arms are a bit full right now." To emphasize the fact Lance shrugs, lifting Kingston's body an inch higher, then lets his shoulders drop back down. Oversight leans forward and flips the switch activating Viper's lamp then falls back a step as Lance again takes the lead and heads for the far door.

CHAPTER 45 - RYKER

Ancient memories of sitting on the couch with a book, something about a little girl and a wolf, come flooding back: memories of his long-dead mother—he is grateful she didn't suffer as much as many—next to him teaching him how to sound out the strange scribbles on the pages. He collapses in front of the panel, crying. He has lost so much to the war—to time. But he has learned to accept that he cannot bring them or anything else back. His face still holds the ability to tear, so he allows himself the luxury of feeling human for a few moments. Then he rises and peers through still-wet eyes at the lights and labels again. He begins sounding out the letters, slowly, painfully at first. The thought of his mother drives him. Then, as sounds once again lock into place with shapes, he reads faster and startles himself when he recognizes a full word. For an instant, he wonders if he felt the same way when he first learned to read, but shakes off the thought and focuses on the task at hand. One word, a long one, takes more time to decipher: "e-n-v-i-envo—e-n-v-I—ENVI!" *What would be the function of envy?* he thinks. *No, that's not it.* He continues. "EnviROnment." The green lights in a row above the label are as bright as the one that goes off in his head when he finally makes sense of the word. He pushes one of the green lamps with a tentative claw. There is a click and he leaps back in fear as the lights in the room go out. He hurriedly stabs the button again. It glows green again and the room lights flicker on again.

Ryker has discovered something important, something he can use to his advantage if the humans decide to storm the room. He wonders why they haven't. Then he goes back to deciphering. Here is a label for generators and another for communications—that one is useless—he lost the power to speak as a result of the mutation. Besides, he doesn't want to talk to the humans. He wants to kill them. There is another label below a row of switches below a bank of blank displays. He flips one of the switches and is rewarded by the screen above it sputtering to life. He peers closer and recognizes the small room he had originally entered. He toggles the second switch and the second monitor flickers to show an elongated creature by a bank of panels. It takes Ryker a few moments of staring to realize he is looking at himself. Somehow, he still thinks of himself as human. This is the first time he sees himself as others see him. He cries out as if stabbed and again breaks down into tears. Still sobbing, he scans the room, looking for the source of the image. A moment later he spots the small black circle embedded into the metal wall near the ceiling. Satisfied, Ryker returns to the displays and flips the remaining switches to see the missile room and a room with desks. A motion on one of the monitors makes him stop and focus. It's a room of old-style beds and humans are in it. His sharp intake of breath startles him as the sound breaks the silence of the control room. He watches the figures move about the room. One is wounded—possibly even dead—Ryker can't be sure, but that knowledge pleases him. One of the other two carries the body. He doesn't understand why humans worry so much about their dead. He has seen enough of death over the past century. He has lost many friends, many family members, until only he is left. *Maybe death is only important to those who have never been around it*, he thinks.

He watches fascinated as the humans search the room. What are they looking for? Maybe someplace to bury the body of the third human. That would explain why they had stopped chasing him. Death is important to humans. Ryker grins. His deformed features would have horrified the humans in his appearance, but also in his thoughts and plans. One human and one overburdened human would be easy targets. Ryker leans over and hits the green buttons throwing the humans and the cameras into darkness. He scans the console, searching. A few minutes of working through the labels brings success. He frowns as he stares at the two key-holes and lone switch above it. He knows about keys. The humans still use them. Once the war had made common electronics only available to the rich in power and government, the few humans still in the wild had resorted to keys to keep the scavengers away from what belongings they had. *The keys, where are they?* he thinks. *They aren't on the console and they aren't on the floor.* He moves to the lone locker and yanks the thin metal door off the hinges. Nothing but dust. *Where are they? I can't kill humans without the human keys.* In rage and frustration, he flings himself at the ancient locker, which topples with a long, loud clang onto the metal floor. A cloud of dust rises into the air and mixes with a metallic tinkle.

For an instant the sound of the air scrubbers becomes labored then settles back to its usual low hum. Ryker looks at the large metal box that now lies in front of him. Triumphant, he retrieves the two pieces of metal that are the target of his ire. He's lucky. The last humans to inhabit this place had tossed the no-longer-needed keys onto the locker, thinking no one would ever need them again, or maybe they just didn't care. Either way, he's found them and needs them.

He fumbles to fit the small objects into the holes. His claws keep getting in the way and he drops the keys twice, letting them slide down the console to be caught by a metal lip that runs around the edge. Several attempts later he has inserted the keys. Satisfied they will not mysteriously slip out, he grasps the leftmost key with the still fleshy parts of his hand and twists it. The key doesn't budge. He tries again with the same result, exerting more pressure. He stares a moment at the obstinate object and tries turning the key in the opposite direction with no more success than the original direction had yielded. He considers twisting the key with all of his might, but fears the key would bend or snap. Ryker decides to try the rightmost key. A moment later, frustration rising, he takes a step back to evaluate another failure. He thinks about slashing the panel with his claws to get to the internal mechanism, but reason tells him the humans who built it probably made it strong enough to withstand simple assaults. His breath rapid, his frustration high, he approaches the console and grasps the two keys. The distance between them would have been impossible for a single human, but he is no longer human. He's even larger than a normal scavenger. "You are special." The memory of his long-dead mother's voice comes flooding into him. He isn't sure it's her voice at this point, but they are her words. That much he does recall.

Both keys yield to his desire to kill. He's not sure why they have, but the button below and between the keys pulses red. A clawed finger reaches for it, hesitates a moment, then the sharp point stabs the button down, piercing it with a satisfying click.

Sirens scream through the complex. Ryker springs back from the console as if it had reached out and bitten him. The noise tears at him and makes thinking clearly difficult, but he consoles himself as he realizes that the pain of the noise is nothing compared to the pain the humans will feel when the missile hits.

The display that had read the mysterious number four blinks rapidly. Four zeroes appear after it. The last two digits change, then change again. He stares at the display, trying to make sense of the strange numbers. Then it hits him. It's the time until the missile launch.

CHAPTER 46 - LANCE

Sirens blare, startling Lance and making him lose his grip on Boomslang. He grapples in the darkness to keep from dropping the man. Next to him, Oversight jumps a foot, his lantern scanning the hallway as he hunts for the unseen assailant. Lance regains control of Kingston's body and curses. Too many things are happening that he can't explain, fewer he can control. He doesn't like the loss of light. He likes the wailing siren less. Gov would have been able to tell him what it means, but Lance is blind and will probably be deaf if the sirens don't stop.

"What the fuck's going on?" Deforest's lamp has ceased its frantic sweep and has settled to a slow nervous scan.

Lance barely hears his teammate over the sirens. He yells back, "Sirens never mean something good is about to happen. Move! We still need to find the med center." Lance stumbles as quickly as he can carry Boomslang to the far end of the hallway and through the open door. Deforest keeps pace with him even as the lantern and his rifle protect their rush from the rear.

The lights don't come on when Lance enters the room. His lamp quickly passes over the room from left to right, top to bottom. He's relieved there are no enemies and more relieved to see medical equipment that is ancient but still recognizable. The war did little to advance medicine. In fact, it did the opposite. Medicine has moved at a crawl and stagnated for most humans. Only the few in power can afford medicine. Fewer still can afford medical research. Gov, however, has made sure the hunter teams are taken care of or, at a minimum, kept them alive. *Shit*, he curses as the siren continues to blare. *Where is Gov when you need him?*

Lance moves to the metal frame of one of the beds. Like the bunks in the other room, any nonmetal or plastic materials disintegrated long ago. The metal lattice creaks as Boomslang's body rolls off of Viper's back and onto it. Viper breathes a sigh and swivels his head to relax the muscles. His relaxation is incomplete. The still-sounding sirens make total relaxation impossible.

Oversight follows close behind. He glances at his unconscious teammate and then focuses back to the open hallway. "Is he going to be alright?"

Lance moves quickly to a cabinet whose glass doors had splintered to the shards that lie on the ground at its base. He pulls open the metal frame of the door by the knobs that remain. The cabinet holds small glass bottles, some shattered, many still intact, but none with the paper labels that originally identified the contents. Lance looks at the bottles then picks up one for a closer inspection. "Shit!" He hurls the gray-filled glass container against the wall. A shower of liquid and glass bounces back at him, which he ignores.

"What's wrong?" Kingston looks over at him in concern.

"I have no idea what any of this stuff is or does. Even if I did, it's all probably useless now." Lance has made another mistake. He was so concerned about getting help for Deforest and finding the med center he has forgotten to take the age of whatever it was he would find into account. *I'm getting old*, he thinks. *I wonder when Gov will realize I'm due for retirement.* He glances at Boomslang, who lies on his back. The gunner's breathing is shallow and he wheezes as he struggles for breath after breath. His skin is gray under Viper's lamp. Oversight stands nervous, fidgeting, gun poised down the hall they had left. Viper has never seen his comms man so nervous. Lance glances from the man on the bed to the man guarding the room. They are all past due being recalled by Gov. Now that the sats are down, he wonders if they ever will be pulled and, if they are, how will the team know? He turns away from the medicine cabinet in disgust and moves quickly over to Boomslang. He still has his mission. He still has to protect and help his team. He rips the bandage off the gunner's arm. The gunner doesn't flinch or otherwise react. The gray pus has dried to a moist, crusty mass, but the infection has changed from red to gray and has spread around the original wound. "Med pack." Viper reaches a hand to Oversight, who tosses him the medical supplies. Viper wastes no time cleaning and dressing the wound. "We're out of antibiotics." He glances at the cabinet and considers trying one of the liquids at random. He's desperate and needs a way to keep the team alive and whole.

Before Viper can act, Oversight interrupts his thoughts. "I see something."

CHAPTER 47 - RYKER

Ryker gives one last look at the display. It reads 3:57:03 and the last two digits flicker every second. He moves to the exit, removes the chair that has done little as a barricade, and yanks the door open. It clangs as it slams into the wall but is no less for wear. He has left the lights on in the storage area adjacent to the control room. He sprints to the door that leads to the hallway and humans. They will be easy to deal with. One is probably dead, the other too occupied with caring for the dead to be much resistance. The one left with the rifle will have to be dealt with first. Ryker enters the bunk room, shutting the door behind him. The room is in the darkness he has created. A light flickers at the edge of the hallway. He hasn't taken into account their hat lights. They aren't as blind or unprepared as he thought they would be. He will have to be more careful, more patient, and more certain before he takes a chance to attack. They may be less dangerous, but even one bullet will be fatal. Ryker scurries to the frame of the opening that leads to the hall. He stoops down on all fours and listens. The humans are yelling but the sirens make understanding and hearing what they say impossible. The screaming sirens grate at him but they signal his revenge. The human light flickers and then fades. Ryker waits a minute to make sure it doesn't return. He sneaks a peek around the corner into the hall. The light moves in a room at the far end. The humans haven't heard or seen him. Ryker settles to the floor at the end of the hallway and waits. The humans will have to sleep. They will be most vulnerable, most unprepared then.

Minutes pass and Ryker shifts as the light at the far end of the room flares an instant before moving on. He lets his breath out slowly. The light blinds him for a moment but he remains still and doesn't give away his location. There are no shouts, no calls of alarm from the humans. He hasn't been spotted. Ryker is getting impatient. What are the humans doing? Why don't they sleep? He considers going back to the room with the displays to see what they are doing, but moving might allow them to escape. He lies still, wishing the sirens would stop their incessant noise. He watches from the relative safety of his position as the lights move about in the back room then stop. The humans have gone to sleep. Ryker waits a long minute to make sure there is no further motion. When none is evident, he rises and rushes the far door.

Light from the human lamps blinds and stuns him. He skitters on the metal floor but continues his dash forward. The humans shout over the sirens. His arm armor is hit but he's too far down the hallway to turn and escape. He's committed and somehow miscalculated. He'd hoped surprising the humans would give him an advantage and allow him to eliminate them quickly and safely. Now he's caught running in a narrow hallway and his only option is a direct assault. More bullets strike him and bounce off. *A lucky shot to the head could as easily kill me as a well aimed one*, he thinks. A bullet ricochets off his armor with a thud, pings from wall to ceiling, and comes to rest behind him. He ignores all of the bullets but still tucks his head lower as he runs. A second more of running and he breaches the humans' room.

His mind takes in the scene in an instant. The dead or injured one lies immobile. The human who had carried him is firing a pistol. The one with the rifle yells something and crouches. The rifle is on the human's shoulder. Ryker sees the muzzle point at his head. Adrenaline surges through Ryker's body as he flings himself at the man. The rifle discharges. Ryker flinches at the muzzle flash and feels the bullet impact his shoulder, twisting him. He hits the human a glancing blow with his body, startling the man and making him lose concentration. The man struggles to bring the rifle up again. Ryker's back is peppered by pistol fire. This isn't what he had planned. The room is too small. The humans had been prepared despite the darkness. Their lamps have undone his plans. Rage fills him. He will not be denied. He slashes at the human's head, his claws flashing in the light of the man's lamp. The man's yelp is audible even above the noise of the sirens. Ryker's attack misses but manages to strike the cursed lamp, which flies through the air to crash against the floor. The light that shone from the human creature's lamp flickers and dies the way the human should have done. The human stumbles back falling against one of the metal bunks. He does not move. The room is darker, but the man with the pistol still fires and yells.

Ryker turns to face the last opponent. The light from the man's head illuminates the fear on the man's face. It's an old face, a gray face, a soon-to-be-dead face. The gun no longer fires, but the human still yells at him. Ryker stands and watches a moment, trying to make sense of the man's screams. The human will scream more once Ryker's claws are done with him. The human flings the pistol at his head but misses. The human is unarmed, ignoring the rifle on his back. Ryker will enjoy this death. He will take his time with this one. Ryker rises up on his back legs and takes a step toward the human. The man's eyes grow large as he stumbles back. Ryker hisses and takes another step forward, playing with his prey. The human's eyes hold terror as they dance, looking for escape. The man steps to the side, away from the injured human on the floor. *Just like a human*, Ryker thinks, *worrying about others instead of himself.* Ryker grins and moves forward. The human has nowhere to run, his back against an old cabinet filled with liquids. It is time to end this. Ryker flings himself at the human, who, snakelike, shifts position. The man's arm darts to a large bottle filled with a clear liquid. The ancient glass smashes over the scavenger's carapace. The liquid splatters over Ryker and for half an instant he's annoyed at the human. Then the pain starts. The burning pain continues and grows. Smoke or maybe steam rises where the liquid touched his armor. That's not where the pain is, however. The liquid has seeped between the plates to his flesh. The liquid burns. *How can liquid burn?* his mind screams. He's hurt. He isn't sure how bad the damage is, but he has survived by not taking chances. He swivels to face the human who had done this to him, swipes at the man with his claws, and hisses. The human dodges away from him. Ryker forgets about killing, dashes through the opening and down the hall, and runs back to the control room as quickly as his body can carry him.

CHAPTER 48 - LANCE

Lance's hand goes to his waist and pulls the pistol up. His head and lamp swivel to the hallway next to Oversight, who kneels by the doorway, his rifle pointing down the metal tunnel. Something catches in the lamplight, then recognition and adrenaline flood him. It's the large scavenger and it's moving fast. Lance pops off a few rounds yelling, "Forget getting the brain! Kill the sucker!" When they had first entered the med center he'd seen there is no escape route. They are trapped and will have to stop the creature and fight it out here.

"Roger! Going for the head." Oversight yells over sirens. "Jeez! Can he move! I can't line up a shot! He changes direction too rapidly to track."

The scavenger closes half the distance. Lance's lamp shows the creature rushing forward then stopping an instant before shifting its position in the corridor before dashing closer. Lance kneels to a shooting position, supporting his pistol arm against the entrance's metal frame. The pistol is as good as a rifle, but not at range. He hopes the close quarters of the corridor make the odds of a lucky shot better. He considers swapping to his rifle, but that would waste precious time and opportunity for a hit.

The nasty is several dozen yards from their location. Beads of sweat form on Lance's forehead. The siren's constant assault and the giant creature's relentless advance are giving him a headache. He fires off two more rounds then reloads, letting the empty magazine bounce on the metal floor under him. Oversight curses, fires, and stops trying to line up a headshot as the creature nears the room. Panic floods through Lance's mind and body. "Pull back!" he yells, standing up and backing away from the entrance. Oversight follows suit and continues firing into the opening. The creature bursts into the room, towering over the two men.

Oversight crouches and manually sights his rifle as he yells, "Shit! He's huge!" The creature turns toward the yelling to face Oversight, its back to

Viper. Viper pulls the pistol up toward the back of the creature's head. The scavenger rushes Oversight just as he fires. Viper, who has never seen a nasty react so rapidly, curses as it shifts its position in midair. Lance sees the creature twist and fling its clawed hand at Deforest, who dodges but stumbles, letting his rifle muzzle drop. Lance fires blindly at the creature's back, trying to draw its attention away from Oversight. The clawed hand swings again and Oversight staggers back. His lamp flies from his head and shatters on the metal floor. Deforest falls backward against one of the empty beds then lies motionless.

Another empty magazine drops from Lance's pistol and he jams a new one in place, brings the weapon up, and fires in a single motion. The creature turns to face him. The pistol fires again then jams. Viper's mind goes blank. He screams at the creature as he tries to force the gun to fire. In desperation he flings the useless weapon at the creature's head as the creature moves forward. *What is it waiting for?* Lance wonders. *Why doesn't it end this?* Lance's mind reengages. He's tired. So tired. His now empty hand touches the pocket where he had lovingly placed the photo. The creature moves a step closer. *It's toying with me,* Lance's brain yells inside his head. *Need to run. Need to get away.* His eyes dart from side to side while he keeps the lamp on his head focused on the creature. Viper's heart beats wildly and his breath is shallow and rapid. His nerves feel like they are trying to rip themselves out of his body. He takes a step to the side. The scavenger blocks the only escape route out of the room. For an instant Lance considers trying to run under the creature's outstretched arms, but the yellow claws that his lamp illuminates dissuade him. Lance's peripheral vision catches sight of a large bottle filled with a clear liquid. Water won't harm the creature, but perhaps smashing the bottle on the creature's head will. Lance's vision locks onto the creature as it moves toward him. He sees it lower itself onto its back legs, preparing to pounce. It uncoils and flies at him. Terror hits Lance before the scavenger does. He ducks and grabs the bottle, swinging it toward the creature's head. Instead, it smashes against an arm, shattering and splattering liquid. Lance's hand jerks back, avoiding the claws and liquid. Lance stands frozen for what seems an eternity, staring at the smoke that exudes from the creature's armor. An instant later the scavenger screams in pain, a scream horrifying in its humanness. The nasty then flees down the corridor into the darkness.

CHAPTER 49 - LANCE

Lance watches the creature disappear from view until his mind reengages. He rushes over to Deforest's crumpled body. He checks the pulse at Deforest's wrist and sighs in relief when he detects a strong, steady pulse. His hand supports Deforest's head as Lance places him gently on a bed. The hand comes away warm and sticky. Lance's lamp lights the blood on his hand. Viper curses, pulls out the med pack from Oversight's belongings, and cleans and dresses the gash where his friend hit his head when he fell. Several minutes of work and Lance allows himself to relax. Oversight will survive, but he'll have a nasty headache. Lance moves to Boomslang. The gunner's face is ashen and haggard in the lamplight. Lance places a hand on the man's forehead. It's cold and the skin is clammy. He glances down at the bandaged arm and flinches. Black tracks have formed and radiate from the wound. Lance checks the med pack and curses again. There is one bandage left and one sanitizer spray canister. He used the last of the antibiotics the last time he dressed the wound. Viper places the pack on Boomslang bed, shines the lamp down the corridor to make sure the scavenger hasn't returned, and then moves back to the cabinet. The smashed glass bottle lies in fragments on the ground. The clear liquid, whatever it was, has evaporated and there is none left. It had hurt the creature. It was a weapon, but a quick scan of the cabinet shows no other bottles with clear liquid in them. Lance also has no way of knowing what the liquid was. The label if, there ever was one, disintegrated long ago.

Lance stands, staring at the cabinet. *So much useless med tech*, he thinks. *They couldn't even bother inventing a useful label.* Yelling, he sweeps an arm across a shelf, flinging bottles off, smashing most; a few hit the floor and roll. He turns his attention back to his team. He has let them down. Oversight will live, but he can't be counted on to defend the room in his state. Boomslang is out and what little hope the room had originally held has disappeared as quickly as the clear liquid had. *I've done this to them*, Lance thinks. *I've failed the mission.*

Realization strikes him and he collapses against the foot of Boomslang's bed. He has failed his friend, teammates, mission, and family. He'd lived and hunted in order to protect them, to protect her. He pulls the photo out and stares down at the face that looks back at him. He sighs. She has probably changed. He knows he has. Time did that, but he's certain she is still as beautiful. *I've failed you, Roxy.* He had promised to return when Gov released them. Now Gov never will and, with his team incapacitated, he won't survive. He mouths a silent "I love you" at the image in his hand and carefully repacks it.

The silence startles him to his feet and he grabs the rifle at his back. His lamp scans the dark room and passes over the two still bodies. The hallway holds no visible menace, no large scavenger with claws. But the sirens have stopped. The silence is a relief. He can now hear and focus on his own thoughts. He lets himself wonder why they stopped. Seeing no imminent threat, he allows the rifle to drop to his side. He walks to the corridor, scanning the darkness. *The only reason the nasty hasn't returned*, he thinks, *is it's hurt, maybe even dying.* It must know it's injured and trapped with no way out except the hall.

A raspy cough pulls Lance to Kingston's side. The light reveals a trickle of dark blood spilling down the gunner's cheek and splattering onto the floor below through the metal mesh of the bed frame. The gunner's skin is ashen and his chest isn't moving. In a panic, Lance grabs the man's wrist and feels for a pulse. His own face turns white in the reflected light. He quickly moves to the other side of the bed and places two fingers along Boomslang's neck. Lance curses under his breath and takes a step back. He looks down at the gunner in silence for a long moment, then reaches down and rips off the "Sharman" name tag from Boomslang's jacket, which he packs reverently with the others he had collected.

He moves to Oversight's side and checks on the young man. Satisfied Oversight is as comfortable as possible and still breathing, Viper slumps down against the cold metal wall. He'd killed them as surely as the scavenger had. He'd failed in the worst way possible. He weeps for his loss and failure, but mostly he weeps for Boomslang until sleep takes him.

CHAPTER 50 - RYKER

Ryker sits in the control room, cringing from the pain that had caused him to flee. He doesn't know what the liquid is, but it hurts in a way he can't recall in his long life. He sits and cowers, flinching at the pain, unable to make it stop or go away. Most of the steam has stopped rising from his armor, but wisps still float ceiling-ward from between the plates. Time passes and the pain is all he knows. His thoughts are a jumble, his pain is constant. His hate now mixes with fear. His rage grows as the pain begins to subside. They had hurt him. They had tried to kill him. They would never have tried were he still human. Humans look after their own kind. He's no longer their kind. The pain subsides to a deep throb that makes him wince as he stands. The pain is now his badge, a reminder of his purpose. The humans, what was left of them, will pay.

He glances at the console. The green display shows 3:03:27 and is still counting down. The sirens still wail and make his head hurt and thoughts fuzzy. He moves to the switches, displays, and buttons, forcing himself to focus through the noise and pain. Reading is still a chore but it comes easier with practice. He finds what he's looking for. He clicks the small metal rod with a claw toggling it into the opposite setting. The count-down continues; the sirens do not. Silence floods the complex, as does his relief from the noise.

He stares at the displays. The one that shows the humans makes him grin. Two of the humans are on the ancient beds while the third is tending to them. The odds are now in his favor. A twinge of pain reminds him of the liquid. The camera, when the humans' light passes over it, shows the cabinet that still holds unbroken bottles. *I won't take another chance,* he thinks. *I'll bide my time. I have the luxury to wait out the human. The human will have to leave the room at some point and, when he does, I'll be waiting.* He settles down on the floor and watches the monitor. The human has settled down as well and has fallen asleep. Ryker perks up. This is the perfect time to attack, but the man holds his rifle across his lap and he's too close to the liquid-filled bottles. Ryker settles down and waits. Pain, stress, and exhaustion bring sleep.

CHAPTER 51 - LANCE

Lance wakes with a start and is instantly alert, his gun up. It takes him a second to recall where he is and what has happened. He checks his watch. He's been asleep almost 30 minutes. He feels refreshed physically, but emotionally he struggles. He checks his teammates. They're down and his options are none. His mistakes have cost them everything. He kicks a leg of the lone metal table as he curses himself. His mind races, trying to find a way to save Oversight and escape the dead-end room they're in. *We're trapped*, his mind screams. *I trapped them. I got Boomslang killed.* Lance stands staring at nothing, breathing hard—he doesn't know how long. His mind engages. *I still have a mission. I have to protect Oversight and get him out safely.* Lance's anger rises again, something he has always been able to control over the years. *I can't get us out until the scavenger is gone, but it can wait us out.* Viper's mind formulates a plan. He will attack the creature before it can attack him. It's hurt, which he knows makes it more dangerous, but he'll have the element of surprise if he can find it.

His lamp scans the room and hall. His nerves tingle through his body as his breathing races. Satisfied there is no imminent danger, he lets himself relax. He sits up against the wall to gather his thoughts and his strength and to plan. He pulls the med kit over to himself and then pushes a pain cap against his leg. He glances at the nearly empty med pack and shoves it to slide across the room to bump against Kingston's bunk. Viper plucks a meal from his pack, rips it open, and downs the contents without tasting anything. *This mission wasn't supposed to go this way. It wasn't supposed to be a repeat of—*. Lance shakes his head to clear the train of thought.

Exhausted and hurting, Lance gets up and walks over to Boomslang's body. He places a hand on Kingston's still chest. "I'm sorry, old friend. I let you down. I shouldn't have taken the chances, made the decisions I did. You and Deforest"—he glances over at his comms teammate—"were always there for me. I wasn't there for you when you needed me. I was supposed to be the team leader." He pauses, then in a quiet voice, as if talking to himself, says, "Some leader I turned out to be." Tears form again and in a loud voice he declares, "I swear I'll get the bastard and do what I can to get you two out of here and to safety." He stands for a moment then checks Deforest. Deforest is still unconscious, but his breathing is regular and obvious.

His face a grim mask, Lance adjusts his pack and steps toward the door. His world spins. The pain cap combined with his fatigue slows his progress and he slumps to the ground. Still conscious, Lance shakes his head and waits for it to clear. He takes a step toward the hallway, then a moment later he second-guesses himself and leans on the edge of Boomslang's bed. He can't leave Oversight unprotected. *What if he goes after the creature and it comes here while I'm searching for it?* Lance's light pierces the hall's darkness. Their supplies are running low. *The creature doesn't have to attack, merely wait for us to starve or die of thirst*, Lance thinks. He and Deforest would both be dead. The storm still raged above. Viper steels himself. At least he has a chance if he can take out the scavenger. He checks Deforest one last time and, satisfied the man is alive and as comfortable as he can be, Viper adjusts the pack on his back and moves out into the hall.

Where would an injured nasty go? he thinks as he enters the abandoned bunk room. It's holed up in the control room, but it hadn't come into the complex that way. Injured, it will probably try to escape the way it had come in. Viper checks the entrance to the storage room with his scope and, satisfied the creature isn't waiting on the other side, enters. His rifle muzzle scans from left to right, up and down. Viper moves across the large chamber. He enters the tall tubular room. *Fuck!* Viper stares up at the missile at the room's center. The catwalks are retracted and white vapor drifts down to where he stands transfixed. Lance shivers; the room wasn't this cold before, was it? Blue-white lights flood the room, making his head lamp useless. He doesn't know much about missiles, but he does know one that is rumbling and appears to be fueling is not a good thing.

Now the sirens make sense, but why had they stopped? Viper shakes himself as if to wake himself from a bad nightmare. If the missile goes up, there is no telling where it would come down, but the damage would make the world, as bad as it was, even worse.

His team is dead. He is dead. The world will be dead if the missile is launched. All thoughts of hunting the scavenger flee his mind. Lance wants to flee—to chase his heart away from this place. He wants to get as far away from the deadly ancient cylinder as he can. He wants to hide. The world had been destroyed by these things. He hadn't lived through it, but he has heard stories, seen ancient pictures that manage to survive. Worst of all, he lives in the aftermath, a world of hunters and scavengers always looking over his shoulder. He'd signed up to help protect the world and those around him. He pulls Roxy's photo out, looks at it a long moment, then replaces it. *I'll never see her again*, he thinks. He failed his team. He failed his mission. He failed her. *The world failed me, but I have to try to save it from becoming worse.* He scans the room with his rifle. *I have to find the control switch or panel. There's none in the silo. The only place it can be is in the control room we passed through.* Cursing, he sets himself. *I have to at least try to stop the missile—or run away terrified.* He has a new mission.

CHAPTER 52 - LANCE

Lance gives the huge missile one last glance, turns, and reenters the storage chamber. He goes through the standard scan protocol as he moves toward the control room, even though the scavenger has probably escaped to the surface. *I've made enough mistakes for three lifetimes*, Lance thinks. *I'm not going to make any more.* He moves quickly and surely but stops when movement through the open door of the control room catches his eye. His scope comes down and he tracks the motion. It's the large scavenger; it hasn't left. *Shit*, Viper curses. His body is covered in sweat and has been ever since he had come across the missile. He wipes his hands, one at a time, on his pants and realigns the scope. The creature has stopped and is beyond the door. In normal circumstances Viper would simply wait out the creature and go for a clean head shot. But there's no way for him to tell what it is up to. If it's wounded and smart, which he now knows it is, it will want to get out of the complex. But it hasn't. Maybe it doesn't know of the shaft his team had entered. *It doesn't matter*, Lance thinks. *The longer I wait the less time I—we have.* His priority is to deactivate the missile, creature or no creature. He stares through the scope, looking for movement. He will have to enter the chamber and deal with the creature.

Lance waits, watching. He doesn't storm the room. Instead he shifts to one side of the door to get a better view of the interior of the control room. The nasty has settled into a far corner of the room; only its armored leg is visible to Viper. He knows the nasty is injured, he's certain of that. But it isn't dead. He doesn't know how badly it's injured. The uncertainty makes Viper cautious. He moves closer, a range that makes using the scope problematic. He flips it and hopes his manual aiming will be good enough. He takes slow, measured steps toward the door and the creature on the floor. His movement is as silent as he can make it; the element of surprise is his. There's no motion from the scavenger. Lance stops, startled by his own loud breath. His heartbeat against his chest is even louder. He'd been in many firefights and been afraid, but this is a terror he's never known. His team is down. He's blind with no intel. He's one human. He's alone. He'd always intellectually understood the dependence each of his team members had on the others. He'd never realized how truly helpless he was on his own. A part of him wonders if the creature feels the same way he does, but he quickly shakes it off as a distraction and weakness. The creature and its kind make human life a struggle. This one has wiped out at least one hunter team on its own. The world will be better off without the creature, especially if it has somehow started the missile sequence. *It must have*, Lance thinks. Nothing he or his men had done could have. He grimaces. The creature is smart, he concludes. Intelligent and large—the combination makes it more dangerous than a normal scavenger. Lance fights to still his rapid breathing.

He flinches but keeps the sight on the creature. It moves. It's still dangerous. Viper slows his breath, trying to still his nerves, which are trying to make him run in terror from the creature, the missile, this place, from life. Concentrating, he forces his breath to slow. His edge smooths; his focus sharpens. He moves forward. He now has a clear view of the creature. It lies on the ground, but its head is blocked by its body. Viper curses. He has no shot. He can wait but waiting can be deadly. He stands, his rifle focused where the head would be had it been in the clear. He has to get the creature's attention while maintaining his shot and what element of surprise he has.

Lance braces the rifle with his chin against his shoulder. With one hand he snakes a food ration from his belt. He won't have a lot of time to react, and he needs the shot to count. He flings the pack against the wall by the control room door. It bounces with a dull thunk. In what seems an instant the creature looks up. Lance grabs the rifle with his now free hand and fires.

The rifle jerks to the left as his freed hand hits it, throwing it and the round wide of its mark. The creature, now fully awake and aware of the human's location, rushes him. Lance fires wildly and without aim. The nasty pounces and strikes him in the chest. His rifle flies out of his hands and slides behind him and out of reach. His breath leaves him with a loud "woof" as he's hit. Ancient terror and reflexes take hold and he kicks and pushes at the large hard body that lies on him. The scavenger is tossed back and lands on all fours, hissing. Viper rolls to his left, anticipating the next attack, and manages to get to his feet, gasping for breath. The creature leaps again just as he reaches the rifle. He swings it by the barrel, striking the creature in the chest. The sound of the impact is as loud as a rifle shot. The creature is caught in mid-leap and rolls across the metal floor to hit an ancient metal canister. The creature regains its footing and faces Viper, who stands panting, holding the rifle like a baseball bat in his hands. He glances from the creature to the control room that holds the missile controls. The scavenger blocks his way. The scavenger is still alive and, although injured, it is still stronger and more agile than he. Screaming, Viper rushes the creature, swinging the rifle with all of his might. The creature, startled by the unexpected rush, backs away on all fours as rapidly as it can into the safety of the control room. Just as Lance reaches it, the metal door swings shut in his face. Gasping for breath, adrenaline filling him, Lance slams the butt of his rifle into the door and curses. "Now what am I supposed to do?"

CHAPTER 53 - RYKER

Ryker wakes with a start. Terror and panic grip him. Instinctively he looks in the direction of the sound as something shatters against the wall above the console. Another cursed bottle. His mind leaps. He catches sight of the human who had shot at him beyond the door. He rushes, slamming into the human and knocking the rifle to the ground. The human screams as he is hit and Ryker knows he's knocked the air out of him. But the human reacts with surprising speed and shoves him away with his feet and hands. Ryker hisses and charges the unarmed human. This will end quickly—and badly for the human, he thinks. However, before Ryker can react, the human has the rifle again and swings it at him. He cringes at the impact and is thrown back. He stumbles to his feet, pain shooting up his side where the blow had struck him and the liquid had penetrated. His vision blurs. He has to escape. The human rushes at him again. Ryker stumbles back through the door and slams it shut before collapsing to the floor in pain. Something pounds against the door. He has lost. His hand goes to the small locket. In pain and exhausted, he sleeps.

Ryker wakes aching. He rolls over and screams in pain. He glances down at his side. There is a long crack, his flesh visible through it. A simple blow shouldn't have been capable of causing so much damage. The liquid must have weakened his armor. Rage fills him. The human had planned it. How else did he know to strike the weakened plates? Now Ryker has two vulnerable areas. *At least I'm alive*, he thinks. He glances at the display. It reads 1:08:13. The pounding at the door has stopped. The human obviously wasn't able to breach the door. *I'm safe*, Ryker thinks. But he is hurt. Fear grips him, tightening his stomach. What if the human has more of the liquid? *He can probably kill me with another blow. I have to flee to the surface. I have to get away from the human.* Ryker stands as the pain flows through his body. He needs to heal. Ryker goes through the door on the opposite side of the control room into the adjoining shaft. He stands and stares up into the darkness a moment then grasps a metal rung above him. He pulls himself up, but pain surges like lightning through his side, causing him to release his grip and fall screaming to the ground.

He lies in the dark shaft, crying, letting the pain ebb. Favoring his uninjured side, he crawls slowly back into the control room, panting from the stabbing pain that comes with every movement. He lies immobile until his breath and nerves calm. He's trapped here in the human structure, unable to escape until he heals enough or dies. It's unfair! Hate fills him. The soft human will probably survive while he dies from cracked armor or starves. He doesn't want to die. A plan forms in his mind. Humans carry medicines and bandages. Maybe he can use them to heal himself. He will have to kill the last human to get the keys to his freedom.

He stays on the floor, exhausted and convulsing. He's alone. He's tired. He has lived longer than he had ever hoped to as a human. *Time is a curse that waits to laugh at you*, he thinks, remembering the saying someone once told him in his youth as a human. He had lived most of his life alone, had never traveled in the other scavengers' packs. He was large. He stood out. He was an easy target. But he had outlasted them all, both in time and in cunning. He had never missed the company of others, but now that he saw his own mortality he yearned to talk to his mother, to hug her, and to be hugged by her. His soul was empty, as was his life. He starts to pull the locket out but hesitates, then withdraws his claw. She is gone. She died from radiation poisoning. Many had. Ryker isn't sure if it was a blessing or a curse. Many had died horribly. Many had been changed—he had. The rich, the powerful, the weak, the poor, all had suffered from the war. But the powerful who held the keys to the government had survived. The insane president had not. He and the capitol had been destroyed in the blast. It had been too easy a death for him. He had escaped the torment with his life. The living had not been that lucky. Ryker had not. His humanity was stolen from him. His friends, family, all that was familiar and known to him, had been taken away in the flash. He'd been an outcast and hunted.

Now he is dying, alone and angrier than he has ever been. The human has done this to him. Humans have done this to him. He glances at the display. 00:47:07. His vengeance will be swift, painless, and merciful. It will come soon. The missile will be vengeful. A missile like the one that is about to launch has taken his life, his reality away. His missile will do the same to the humans who hunted him and his kind: eye for eye, claw for bullet, missile for missile. Ryker makes noises that pass for laughter since he's no longer capable of human laughter. He's alone, but he has a missile. He's alone, apart from the human. He will deal with the creature, find the medical pack, heal himself, and make his escape to watch the artificial sun. Satisfied, he sighs.

CHAPTER 54 - LANCE

Lance checks on Oversight. Deforest is still unconscious but seems otherwise okay. There isn't anything he can do about Boomslang's body. He can't take it out of the complex and he doesn't have anything with which to cover him. Lance swallows hard as he glances at the large man who lies cold and still far from his home. Lance knows Boomslang didn't have any family and had been a scavenger hunter longer than he had been. Lance exhales a long, slow breath. He's been through this before. The memory tightens his stomach. It has happened before, but previously it was his team leader who had lay dying. Lance crumples against the cold wall, burying his face in the crook of his elbow. They had told him he'd done all he could, but Jim had still died. *I let him die. I should have shot the scavenger when I had the chance,* Lance thinks for the countless time. He had failed the team then. He has failed his team now. Now he's the team leader. Now it's worse. Several minutes later he stands. His eyes are red, his sleeve wet.

Viper turns away from his team and moves back to the storage chamber. His lamp flickers. He curses, realizing he's been using it full time since they entered the complex and it hasn't had a recharge cycle in the sun. The lamp isn't going to last much longer now that the complex's lights have gone out. He checks the ammo he has left and collects the little that Boomslang had. He lets Oversight keep his in case he wakes and needs it. Lance looks at the shells in his hand. He has enough for one full clip. That should be enough if he's careful and lucky. He moves among the pillars and debris back toward the control room. The creature knows he is alive and after it. If it's smart, it will stay barricaded in the only place he knows of that could stop the missile. His rifle won't penetrate the walls or door of the room; he has to find some other way to breach the door. He considers going up the second shaft and back down the way they had originally come in to circle around. But he doesn't know if the storm is still overhead. He won't last a minute if it is, and going up to determine if it has passed or not will waste precious time.

Somehow he has to lure the creature out of the room. Viper's dimming light scans the debris and ancient metal canisters, searching for anything he can use. He spots a cluster of large canisters in one corner of the storage area that his team had not explored. He moves quickly to it and examines the containers. They're old but solid. What lettering there may have been on them is long gone. The tops are sealed with metal-rimmed lids that clasp down onto the body of the canister. Lance looks around the area, making sure the creature is nowhere to be seen before he leans his rife against one of the canisters. Grasping a clamp in each hand, Viper pulls up and is rewarded by a loud snap as the clasps break their ancient hold and fly up. The lid is soon removed and Lance aims his lamp into the dark interior of the container. It's empty apart from a small pile of debris and dust at its bottom. The second container yields the same. The third attempt rewards him with a long, oddly shaped piece of steel. He lifts it out and holds it in his hands. It's heavy. He has no idea what it was originally for, but as he swings it, it easily dents one of the containers. He gives the hunk of steel a pat and sets it next to his rifle. The last container holds nothing usable. He turns back to his rifle and the metal he had found when the lamp on his hat flickers, blinks once, then goes out, leaving him in pitch-black darkness. Cursing, he grabs the rod, his heart beating rapidly.

CHAPTER 55 - LANCE

The echoing sound of a door being flung open jars his attention to the control room. Lance shoves the rod into a loop on his backpack. His pulse quickens. He crouches and brings his rifle up, waiting. He doesn't have to wait long. The sound of the creature's claws against the metal floor make click-clacking noises as it runs. Both of them are now in darkness, but Lance has the advantage. As long as he doesn't move or make noise to attract attention, he can track the creature by the sound it makes. It isn't trying to be quiet. The scavenger runs across Viper's path, heading toward the med center where his team lies. "Shit!" Viper curses under his breath. *I killed Kingston*, he thinks. *I'm not going to kill Deforest.* Yelling at the top of his lungs, he springs from his hiding spot and rushes toward the click-clack of the creature's movements. As he approaches he fires blindly. Lance knows if he manages to hit and kill the creature, it will be a lucky shot; he's trying to pull the creature from his team.

The creature stops and Viper can no longer hear its steps. He continues forward, yelling and firing as he goes. The muzzle flash illuminates the area in front of him. As he moves he catches sight of the creature, which is up on its back legs, its vulnerable head high above Lance's line of fire. He continues his rush, firing. The gun starts making click-click sounds. The clip is empty, but the creature has seen him and he it. He curses it, the darkness, and being alone without support. He tosses his rifle to his right as he closes the gap to the scavenger and pulls the hunk of metal from the loop on his back. He grabs one end of the steel implement and swings it through the darkness in front of him. He hits air. He catches himself from being pulled off his feet by the inertia of the swing as pain rips through the flesh at his hip and he falls rather than sees the creature bound past him. Viper ignores the burning pain of the pulled muscle, swings again, and again misses. He turns and braces himself with the metal rod held in front of him vertically. Something hits the bar at waist height, almost wresting it from his grasp. He pivots the bar upward and is rewarded by the tip of his weapon hitting something solid. A hiss in the pitch-black room grabs his attention. He shifts and swings at the sound with all of his might. The bar whooshes through the darkness, hitting nothing. He swings again and feels the metal implement stop in mid-swing with a thud. The silence is shattered by a scream. He's hurt the scavenger. Viper stands, panting from the exertion, his eyes darting from side to side, seeing nothing. The creature isn't moving. He doesn't hear the claws of its feet. Its scream has faded into the silence.

Viper freezes, trying to still his breathing, his eyes darting from side to side, listening for the slightest sound that isn't his. The darkness feels like it's pressing in on him. He doesn't know how sharp the creature's night vision is but it hasn't attacked, which hints it's as bad as his or worse. His heart pounds against his chest and blood pounds in his ears. Where is it? What's it doing? He shifts his head to cover more area around him without turning his body. The bar in his hands is heavy, but he keeps it raised in front of him both to remain silent as well as to protect his head and chest. Beads of sweat form on his forehead and begin to roll down into his eyes. He fights the urge to wipe them and instead blinks them away. He tastes salt as he licks his lips. He hasn't eaten or had anything to drink in a while. It will be a while before he has a chance to do so, and he has more important concerns. His shoulder itches and his hip burns in pain. The darkness is complete. Without his lamp he can't make out the metal object he holds a few inches from his face.

The scavenger hisses to his left, but before he can react he's thrown to the ground, his makeshift weapon skittering into the darkness. He strikes out with hands and feet in a flurry driven by panic and survival instinct long suppressed but not forgotten by his body. He pounds the dark shape on top of him with his fists, kicking with his boots while screaming at the top of his lungs. Adrenaline pumps into him replacing fear and thought with strength and speed. His attacks land, but he has no way of telling whether they are effective. The creature hisses and strikes at him, but Viper ignores the attacks, instead fighting with all the strength and reflexes he has. Something slams into his head, lighting the darkness with sparks and moving lights. His ears ring and he feels himself falling. *Shit,* he thinks as his senses leave him.

CHAPTER 56 - RYKER

Ryker falls back in the darkness. His hand goes to his side where the human had hit it. He's injured badly. He underestimated the human and his resourcefulness, but he killed the human who now lies on the ground beside him, and that alone is worth the pain. He stands in the darkness, struggling to regain his breath. His plan to attack the human had failed when the human's light went out. He had counted on it to let him find the creature, and being thrown into darkness had made his attacks random and unfocused, but he had come out victorious. The human is dead, but there is little satisfaction Now, he can find the med packs and tend to his wounds. First he has to turn the lights on again since there's no longer a need for stealth or darkness. He has won. He makes his way slowly and in pain back to the control room. A glance at the display shows 00:11:08. *I've won*, his mind repeats. *I'll have my revenge against all humans. I can rest then.* He flicks switches with a claw and the complex is again flooded with light. It's time to find the medicine.

He goes on all fours back into the storage area. His side hurts and liquid oozes from between his plates. *That's not a good sign*, he thinks. The plate on his side is crushed. He's exhausted and in pain. His progress is slow as he moves past pillars and debris to where he had killed the human. He stops short, confused. This is where the body should be, but there is no body. *Maybe I'm confused. Maybe it's somewhere else. It was dark*, he tells himself as he scans the now-lit area around him. He hisses at the sight of the canisters he had originally seen the human near when the lamp went out. The human's rifle lies several yards away. Ryker crouches lower and spins in place, searching the room. There's no body, no human. He hasn't killed it. Now it is wounded and dangerous and once again loose in the complex. *It will head back to be with its own kind in the room with the bottles*, Ryker thinks. His hatred for the lone human grows as does the pain in his side. He crumples to the ground in a spasm of pain. The hurt passes a minute later; his hatred does not. Steeling himself, he rises on all fours and walks slowly toward the room with the humans. He knows the human is wounded. It was unconscious when he left it. It's in pain. It's probably confused and unfocused. He won't underestimate it again. It probably went back to heal and get the weapons from its dead kin. Ryker pauses, letting his pain subside. He can't afford another mistake. Even injured, he's stronger than an unarmed human, but the human won't be expecting an attack so quickly. He moves to the entrance of the bunk room, pausing to let the pain fade again. Moving makes it flare like a white-hot flame in his side. *I'll be able to rest and heal once I've killed the human.* He will either kill him or die trying.

CHAPTER 57 - LANCE

Lance regains consciousness and rolls over slowly. His leg is limp and doesn't respond, and he realizes the nasty sliced through the bone. He curses his own clumsiness that caused the injury. The pain in his head is excruciating. His eyes tear as he sits, remembering what had occurred. His gaze darts around, looking for signs of his enemy as he reaches back for his rifle and curses. He'd cast it aside in favor of the metal instrument. On hands and one knee, he feels the area around him, fighting the pain as he searches for the bar. *I need a weapon*, he thinks as he strains to hear the scavenger. How long had he been unconscious? He glances at his watch. At his best guess, he was out a few minutes. He continues searching the floor and is rewarded when his hand clasps the makeshift weapon. The pain in his head makes thought and concentration hard. The pain in his leg makes walking impossible. Lance leverages himself up on the weapon until he stands. The rod makes a poor crutch, but it will have to do.

Lance looks around, trying to get his bearings. The velvet darkness that enrobes him yields no hints to the direction he's facing, much less where in the large storage area he is. The darkness hides the columns, the doors, and the creature. A shiver runs down his spine. The blackness goes in and out of focus as his head spins. His stomach growls, startling him. He curses. His stomach is enough to betray him. The only other sounds he hears are his heart and heavy breathing along with the low hum of the air circulators. He stands panting, thinking, *I need a more defensible location*. He tries resetting the lamp on his hat, to no avail. The battery has drained and without sunlight it's useless. He stands bathed in the pain of his head and leg, leaning against his crutch. A plan of sorts forms in his frazzled mind. He'll find a wall and follow it until he comes to a door. How many were there? Three? Four? He can't recall clearly through the pain. *Maybe I'm already dead: alone, blind, lost, and in pain.* Lance shakes his head to clear the thought he knows is false and distracts him from escaping the situation. The movement of his head causes the pain to spike, makes him more dizzy, and elicits a small whimper from his parched lips. *Well, I won't do that again any time soon,* he concludes once the pain and dizziness recede to tolerable levels. Lance takes a deep breath, steadies and steels himself, and hobbles forward. He would either run into something, like the nasty, or a wall.

His progress is slow and painful, and he almost trips over piles of debris several times along the way. The darkness is uniform to such an extent he almost runs into one of the pillars had his makeshift crutch not clanked against it as he moved forward. He continues to walk in what he thinks is a straight line, the tip of the metal object clinking against the metal floor as he moves in a slow rhythm. Confused, he stops. The sound of the rod echoes the sound of the creature's claws. He stands frozen, then proceeds once he's certain the clinking he heard was that of the metal and not a claw. The pain in his leg burns. The pain in his head waxes and wanes with his movements. His vision would have been blurry had he been able to see. He stops frequently, both to let the pain subside and to regain his breath. Lance sweats profusely now and his nerves are on edge, anticipating an attack at any instant.

He glances around in the darkness. Lance has been afraid many times in his life, but this is the first time the fear threatened his existence. This was the first time he had ever been at such a disadvantage. Always before he had had his team for support. He had firepower. He had sight. He was never alone. Now he is isolated. The fear is personal now. The ancient missile silo that smelled of dust, decay, and his own sweat could become his grave. He pauses his trek to find the wall, stunned as realization hits him. *I could die here. No one would know. No one would care.* His fingers fumble at his pack and retrieve the image. He stares at it in the darkness that hides it from his sight. He imagines Roxy in his mind. He knows it's the Roxy he left. She has most certainly changed, as has he. He loves her still; he imagines she still loves him despite the years, despite the distance, despite his betrayal. He misses her. Every night before going to sleep he had spoken a quiet goodnight to her, hoping she would hear him and take comfort in the knowledge he was protecting them by hunting. If he died, she would never know. With sats down, Gov had no way to track them. A thought collapses him where he stands. Would Gov tell her of his death if he could? What if she was already dead? Would Gov have told him? He thought back, trying to recall hearing if other hunters had been told about the death of a loved one. Lance had always assumed it happened because everyone said Gov would. He sat panting. He couldn't remember a single instance or story where it had occurred.

Viper sits in the darkness, clasping the metal object across his chest. It's little comfort. His confused mind searches for answers to questions he's afraid to ask but asks nonetheless. Why would Gov keep the information about the death of a loved one a secret from the hunters? Why hadn't Gov recalled the team years ago? They are overdue for retrieval. Who is Gov? But mostly his mind keeps asking, *Is Roxy dead?* After several minutes of sitting the pain in his leg forces him back up onto his crutch. He stumbles forward, hoping to find the wall. Several steps later he comes across it. He stands a moment, then chooses a direction at random and moves along the wall, searching for an entrance. The room floods with light, which blinds him in a way the darkness hadn't. Panicked, he grasps the rod tighter, swiveling in a circle, expecting an attack. None comes and his vision slowly clears. Why had the lights come on? A part of him replies, *the creature.* Lance is lightheaded, dizzy, but he moves forward. A door comes into view. His pace slows. Weak and disoriented, he knows he has to reach it. His hand touches the metal frame of the opening. Exhausted, he pulls open the door and falls through.

CHAPTER 58 - RYKER

Ryker freezes at the entrance to the bunk room. A dull thud catches his attention, drawing him back into the storage area. He moves as quickly and purposefully as his injuries allow. The human must have decided to escape instead of going back to his own kind. Ryker will put an end to him once and for all. The sound doesn't repeat, but there are only two other entrances to the storage room. *The human didn't pass me on the way to the control center, so he must be moving to the other shaft*, Ryker thinks as he heads in the direction of the door closest to him. Ryker pauses to examine the trail of blood along the wall that leads to the door. Despite his pain, Ryker grins. The human had started bleeding somewhere between where Ryker had injured him and the wall. It will be easy finding him now. Ryker resumes his hunt, more certain now of the human's location. If he is lucky, the human will be weak from the loss of blood.

Forgetting his own pain, Ryker begins to lope, then collapses as the injuries in his side override all thought, all movement. Even the desire to scream is shut down. He is all pain, a white-hot pain that sears through his mind and body. He lies, panting and helpless, yards from the doorway. His body twitches involuntarily, his nerves and muscles no longer under his control. He isn't sure how long he lies this way, incapacitated and alone, but in what seems like an eternity, the pain and twitching subside. His mind forms thoughts; his senses accept normal inputs again. A short time later he stands, stifling a scream from the pain as he moves toward the door and the human. Weakness slows him. Ryker pushes onward, driven by the thought the human is in a worse condition. He has to take advantage of the situation and finish this. He can rest and heal after the human is dead. He crosses the remaining yards in pain and slower than he wants, but moving faster just makes the barely tolerable pain intolerable. He pauses to the side of the open door, gathering his strength and wits.

He will end the life of this human. Then the missile will end many more. He will be avenged. They will know what it is like to lose one's life, love, and humanity. He stands a long time. *What if I die? What if the human gets lucky again? I have to see my vengeance through. I won't die. I've lived longer than any human has, and longer than any scavenger I've known. I'm immortal. Pain is the price of my immortality. I'm tired. I want to lie down and sleep.*

Ryker's side throbs, but he has to kill the human. He has to end this so he can heal, rest, sleep, and go home. His memory flashes back to his home, his mother, the sun that came through the window in the kitchen as she baked. He misses her. He wants to go home. He was too young to go down the street on his own. That's what his mother had said. Then the flash had come. His mother had screamed, then she had stopped moving. He had gone out on his own down the street to find help. But there was none. Everyone was screaming and running. He remembers climbing into a sewer pipe and crying when the air started to burn. When he woke up he had changed.

He wants to cry now, but anger prevents him. He had learned to survive by eating disgusting grubs, worms, anything he could find. Ryker tries to remember the taste of his mother's cooking, but the memory had left him long ago. His claw goes to the locket, something she had given him on his last birthday with her. He had had many birthdays since, but none had held any meaning. Ryker's heart is ready to burst. He was just a child. How could they do this to him?

The sorrow pulls him down into despair lower than he has ever known; his hate flares to the highest it has ever been. His injuries, his pain, vanish in the white-hot hate he feels for humans. Now one of them had hurt him—hurt him badly. His eyes dart to the open doorway. His hate sharpens his focus and vision. The edges of the metal frame are more solid, the colors more vivid. The hum of the air recirculators is more intense. The human's not visible, but the trail of smeared blood says he's near. There will be more of the human blood if Ryker has anything to say about it.

CHAPTER 59 - LANCE

Lance drags himself up, using the metal rod for leverage, and leans back against the wall to rest. He needs rest. He needs sleep. He has failed everyone and everything important to him. He fights to calm his nerves and breathing as he looks up at the missile. His breath catches. Lance has no idea when it will launch or even if it will, but he couldn't chance it not going off. His priority now is one of the most basic instincts a human has—survival.

Now that the lights are on, he takes a moment to survey his injuries. He grimaces at the bone visible through the sliced muscle and tendon of his leg. The creature hadn't sliced through the bone as he had originally thought, but the leg was for all intents dead with no control. The scavenger's claws had torn through his armor as a hot knife through butter. Gov had provided all of his team's gear. Gov would have known a scavenger's claws would penetrate the armor. Why had Gov given them inferior defenses? His mind races with questions, but the answers are beyond him. He feels the back of his head, flinching. The moist, warm blood, matted hair, and dent in his skull tell him he has struck something or something has struck him. He'd slammed his head against the floor when he fell. There is no indication of a claw cut. His body armor has multiple gashes, tears, and cuts, but he's lucky nothing penetrated.

As he takes a step toward the missile, he thinks of his team and Roxy. He has no idea how to stop the launch, but he knows where it can be done—the control room. *I have to get to it to find how to abort the launch and save everyone—save Roxy.* His head swims and he staggers forward, clutching his crutch to maintain his balance.

A sound on the opposite wall grabs and focuses his attention. He plasters himself flat against the wall, gripping the iron rod in both hands. The clicking of his crutch stops. He holds his breath and waits. The click-clacking of claws on metal tells him the scavenger is approaching. Furtively, his vision scans the missile room looking for another weapon, but the silo is empty apart from the missile and support equipment, which is too large for him to use. His focus returns to the sounds outside, which have stopped. The creature knows he's here. The trail of blood he left is easy enough to follow.

Viper's weak and injured. So is the scavenger. He had wounded it. *I can kill it*, he thinks. *I have to conserve my strength and energy. I'll wait and rest until the nasty comes through, then attack before it has time to react.* A warm bead of sweat or blood trickles down the back of his neck; he doesn't know which. Lance tilts his head back to force the liquid into his collar. The motion makes his head and thoughts spin again. The pain throbs. *I probably have a concussion.* Viper takes deep, slow breaths to clear his head and vision, but only partially succeeds.

Viper's attention goes back to the creature outside. Why is it waiting? Why doesn't it come in? A blast of venting propellant makes him glance at the large missile. Then it hits him. The creature is waiting for the launch. He doesn't know why. Viper doesn't care, but he knows that if the creature is waiting for the launch, it's going to be soon and not good for him or what was left of the country. His heart pounds. He isn't old enough to have lived through the Gaman war, but he's heard the stories and seen what images had survived. Another missile. Another war. He gulps. His mouth is suddenly dry.

He had never admitted to his fears, but he had them. Every time he went on a mission, every time he was in a firefight, every time he made a decision, the fear was there. He was afraid of making a mistake, of failing a mission, of losing his team, and, most of all, of dying. He had been on missions and firefights and survived them all. He had made decisions and had now lost his team and his own life hung by a thread. Everything had had a price. He failed his primary mission of keeping his team alive and safe. If the missile went up, he would have failed his most important mission: keeping Roxy safe. Viper wipes the tears from his eyes. He's weak. He's older than most hunter team leaders and he's a failure. The cost is too high. He should have been recalled years ago but he had believed Gov knew what Gov was doing. He wonders if his trust in Gov has been misplaced. Gov had let them down. Gov had failed them. Lance wants to go home. He wants his team whole. He wants to be in Roxy's arms again. He has paid and paid dearly.

What is the nasty doing? Why is it waiting? his mind asks again, and again the answer comes back: *the missile.* His mind snaps back to the silence. Viper has to stop the missile. Even without Gov's guidance and his team's support, he knows he has to prevent the carnage the missile will wreck.

I have to save Roxy. But what if I fail? What if I make a mistake again? What if the creature kills me? His mind races over possibilities and reasons not to act. The bud in his ear has been silent since his team had gone down. He keys it once, hoping to get an answering click from Oversight or Boomslang—then remembers Boomslang is dead. There's no answering click. A deep sadness and depression fills Lance, an emptiness of hope and support that verges on hysteria. There's no one and nothing that can help him. He slides, his back against the wall, down onto the floor. All concern for the scavenger that bided its time outside the silo is gone. It doesn't exist. Only he, Lance, exists in his suffering.

A loud hiss brings him back to reality. He springs up, pain shooting through his leg, bracing himself against the wall, the metal rod at the ready. He allows himself a deep breath when he realizes propellant has vented again. The missile's background sounds rise to a low rumble. *It's preparing to launch*, he thinks. Fear and panic grip Lance. He freezes, torn between the panic and fear. His mind repeats a single thought, *Roxy... Roxy... I have to save her. I might fail, but if I don't try, I most certainly will fail.* He will die trying. Grasping his makeshift weapon and screaming, Viper limps toward the door.

CHAPTER 60 - RYKER / LANCE

A human scream breaks Ryker's reverie. He freezes a moment as his attention shifts back to the door and he sees the human rushing at him, brandishing a metal rod. Blood streams down the human's face and he struggles, but he moves rapidly. Ryker's exhaustion disappears as adrenaline floods his body and survival kicks in. He leaps and crashes into the human before the man has a chance to swing the metal club. The two combatants crash to the ground, grappling and wrestling to control the metal rod between them. Ryker's impact cuts off the human's scream. Viper maintains his grasp on the rod, but Ryker's claws wrap around the metal and yank it, pulling the human's face close to his own. Lance grimaces at the stench that exudes from the creature's mouth. Lance changes tactics and slams the rod forward into the creature's chest. Surprised by the change in direction, Ryker's own momentum plus that of the rod and Viper flings him back, twisting the rod out of the human's hands.

Ryker's clawed hands fumble with the weapon, but he manages to steady it. The human stumbles backward when his grip on the rod fails. Ryker sees fear in the human's eyes. *I should be feared. I'm big. I'm strong. I'm eternal,* Ryker repeats in his mind. Ryker advances, fighting to hold the rod. Frustrated and angry, he gives up trying to fight the rod and flings it at the human. Lance's eyes grow wide as the hunk of metal hurtles at him, end over end. He steps aside, but his leg gives way and he collapses on the floor as his weapon bounces noisily into the missile silo. Pain shoots up his leg and into his brain, but Lance's resolve is firm. He fights it and manages to lunge forward on one knee toward the creature as it rushes him. Lance's arms encircle the armored legs of the scavenger who trips and crashes to the ground. Ryker's impact with the ground jars

Lance's already injured head. His vision blurs and goes red. He wills himself to stay conscious and continues to entangle the scavenger's legs.

Ryker hits the floor and is briefly stunned by the impact, then realizes the human has his legs in a hold. Ryker tries to twist onto his back, but the human's grip is firm and Ryker only manages to get onto his wounded side. Ryker screams and slashes at the human at his feet, but his arms can't reach the creature. He begins kicking and thrashing his legs to force the human off, breaking the human's hold. Ryker's clawed foot catches the human's hand as it moves away. The human screams, grabbing the wounded hand that now drips blood.

Lance stares at the blood pooling in his palm. His mind shuts the pain down after the initial razor sharp cut, then goes into flight mode, silencing all other options. *I have to get away. I have to survive. I don't want to die*, he thinks. He drags himself away from the creature that lies next to him and moves as quickly as he can to the missile silo. A dark red smear of blood trails behind him as he uses his injured hand to crawl to safety.

Ryker, free of the human, lies in pain, whimpering. His side feels as if it's on fire, but he has been lucky. He's survived. He's fought off the human—at least for now. Gasping for breath, he watches the human pull itself across the floor into the room with the missile. *It's just another wounded animal now*, he thinks. Ryker lies on the cold metal floor, resting, gathering his strength and will. He rolls over onto all fours, fighting the pain. *I can't let the human recover. I have to kill it while it's hurt.* Ryker takes a step forward and collapses in pain. He lies panting. *I'm exposed and vulnerable if the human comes back with the metal thing.* Gasping as pain wracks his body and brain, he stands again. He moves forward unsteadily. He has one goal and that's to survive, but to do that he has to kill the human. He stumbles forward one slow, painful step after another.

Lance crawls into the missile silo, weak and increasingly disoriented. His blurred vision catches sight of the metal rod. He grasps the weapon then releases it with a yelp. Blood drips from the hand onto the weapon and floor. He glances behind him as a slow, irregular click-clacking tells him the creature is coming. Cursing to himself, he grabs the rod with his uninjured hand and leverages himself up to use the heavy metal and his good leg to push himself back against the wall. It's a slow, painful process, but he manages to sit up still holding the bar.

Lance's breath is shallow and fast. His head hurts and his vision is blurred and swims. Lance's energy wanes. His hand and leg drip blood. He's lost a lot. He wants to rest, to sleep. He wills himself to focus and remain awake. He can't make a mistake now, not now. A sudden calmness comes over him. He isn't sure if it's the endorphins kicking in or the loss of blood, but he feels warm and at peace. *I'm dying*, his mind tells him. The fear and terror leave him and he knows what he has to do. He will kill the creature—the effort will probably kill him. At least Deforest will survive. He'll save the rest of his team. The huge metal cylinder in the center of the silo begins to rumble and a new siren begins to blare.

CHAPTER 61 - LANCE / RYKER

Ryker cringes at the sudden sound of the siren. What had the human done? He pushes the pain aside, gathering the last of his strength, and rushes through the door on all fours. He has to stop the human. The human must not be allowed to spoil his vengeance. Something smashes into his back, forcing him flat onto the ground. Screaming in rage and pain, he rolls over onto his back, flailing at what had hit him. The human is on his knees, holding the metal thing aloft. Ryker rolls as the weapon comes down again, barely missing his hand as it strikes the floor with a clang loud enough to compete with the wail of the siren. Hissing, he pushes himself off his legs at the human, who appears stunned by the impact but manages to hold onto the rod.

Electric pain shoots up Lance's body as metal hits metal. He'd sat waiting with the rod poised high when the creature had come skittering though the door. He'd slammed the creature to the ground but had missed on the second swing. He blinks the tears of pain out of his eyes just in time to see the scavenger rush him despite its visible injuries. Despite his own pain, Lance shifts on his good knee enough so the creature only catches him with a glancing blow of its body. This is enough, however, to throw Lance off balance and onto the floor. He clutches his weapon like a dead man clutching at life. He rolls as the creature follows up with a swipe of its claws. The next swipe Lance blocks with the rod despite being on his back.

Ryker hisses again as his shoulder slams into the human's arm. The human falls over from its crawling position onto its back. The wound in the human's leg is raw with dark and dried blood, the bone visible. He'd hurt the human badly during the last attack. Ryker swipes at the already injured leg, but the human rolls away. He swings again, this time at the human's face, but all he hits is the metal of the creature's weapon. Before he can react, the human pivots the rod and its end strikes his injured side.

Panting, Viper struggles to hold on to the rod as he blocks the slash. He quickly brings the far end of the long rod up, hitting the nasty's cracked side armor. A scream of pain drowns out the siren and low rumble of the missile behind them. Viper follows up the blow by rotating the rod in his hands to bring the near end up into the creature's throat.

Ryker screams as the rod slams into his side. He ignores the pain and forces himself closer to the human, but the human moves the pole and the other end slams into the armor plate at his collar. An inch higher and he wouldn't have recovered. As it is, the impact freezes him for an instant. The human adjusts and Ryker sees the end of the weapon circle and target his head.

Viper's attack makes his hands ache, but he ignores them because his other injuries coupled with the blare of the siren make the sting in his hands nonexistent. His adrenalin is maxed out and he's exhausted. Viper circles the near end of his weapon away from the armor it had struck and toward the creature's face. He shoves the rod forward with all of his might.

The dull end of the metal thing moves toward his face and Ryker instinctively closes his eyes, pulls back, and throws up his hands. He's surprised when no impact comes and he feels the rod between his hands. His eyes open and he sees the human struggling to push the rod toward his face, but he is strong. He is stronger than the human despite his own injuries and pain. Ryker intertwines his hands and claws around the metal bar, hissing as he does. He twists the bar between his hands. The human yelps in surprise and pain.

Viper gasps as he loses his grasp on the weapon and is thrown toward the missile as the creature twists the rod. Gasping for breath, Lance gets on his knees and sees the creature fling the metal rod aside. His head hurts. His leg hurts. He is losing blood. His vision is blurred. He just wants to sleep, to rest, to be in Roxy's arms again.

Ryker's movement has wrested the weapon from the human, but his hands are too clumsy and his claws get in the way of wielding it the way the human can. He flings the useless thing aside, confident it will cause him no further harm. The human sits near the missile, panting. His eyes are glazed and there are growing pools of blood. The human supports himself with his hands on the floor in front of him. Ryker grins as he gathers his breath. He has won. He will finally get the vengeance he has desired all of these years. He forces himself up on all fours, gathering what energy and will he has left.

Lance gulps, his mouth dry. He's panting and, in one last attempt, remembers to trigger the bud that is still in his ear. "Oversight. Oversight. Do you copy?"

Ryker's breath is fast and ragged. He stands and watches. The human speaks to himself, praying. Humans, he vaguely remembers, have gods. He will allow the luxury for it means the human knows he is about to die.

"Oversight," Viper repeats. "Do you copy? SH-3, do you copy? SH-2? Are you there? I need backup."

Ryker can't make out the words. The human mumbles. He looks scared. He looks horrified. He looks desperate. Ryker doesn't believe in gods. Humans have taken his humanity away. Only humans need gods. He leaps.

Lance curses. There is no response. He is alone. The next second the creature is on him and he is pushing it away with his hands, but his strength is waning. The creature swipes and hits his side through his body armor. The new pain causes him to scream. He pummels the scavenger, striking the nasty's hard shell with his bare fists.

The human strikes him but only lands blows on his body with his soft hands. *I am strong*, Ryker thinks. Human fists are no match for his armor, even though damaged. He slashes and claws, striking the human's covering over and over. The human moves slower and slower, his punches weaker and more frantic. Ryker hisses and looks into the human's glazed eyes and hisses again.

Viper's knuckles are bloody but his hands have had no impact on the creature or its armored plates. The scavenger is winning, shredding through his armor and through his body. He feels himself fading away. All thought leaves him and only the desire to live remains. The creature's body presses on him, its eyes peering into his. The nasty's eyes are blue. Some part of Lance, detached and far away, wonders why the scavenger has blue eyes. His subconscious screams, "Live!" His left arm is not pinned under the creature's weight. He struggles to get it to move where he wants it to go.

Ryker lies panting on the human, using what energy he has left trying to tear the human to pieces. The human fights, but only with one arm. The human lands a blow on his face, the pain stinging him and making him howl.

Lance's fist lands on the creature's head and it howls in pain. Lance's hand moves down to his waist and fumbles, searching.

Ryker recovers and swings at the arm, but he's weak and the claws miss the arm that moves to the human's side.

Viper's free hand finally grasps the knife at his belt and he wills the exhausted muscles to draw it.

Ryker pushes himself up with his hands in order to more easily slash the human's head. The rumble in the room around them rises, drowning out the wailing siren as well as their struggle.

He glances away from the human toward the sound. A faint smile forms on his mouth.

Viper summons the last of his energy and thrusts the knife up and into the creature's exposed throat. Blood gushes from the wound and down his arm.

Ryker manages a howl as he clutches at his throat, falling to the side and off the human.

Lance lets his injured head drop to the floor. He lies, gasping for breath. He's won. He's saved his team. He's completed his mission. The scavenger lies next to him, squirming and trying to staunch the flow of its blood.

Ryker grapples with the wound at his neck, but he has won. He's exacted his revenge. His movement subsides but the pain and bleeding do not. The human doesn't, but he doesn't care. He has won. Fear hits Ryker; the fear of being alone. Death is coming. He is afraid. He uses the last of his energy to draw the locket from his pouch.

Lance lies fighting to remain awake and conscious as what is left of his energy drains out of him. The mission is a success. He's won. He's saved his team. His thoughts turn to home and Roxy. He's saved her. He's at peace. He's done all he could do. Lance lets out a long, slow breath when he thinks he hears the creature beside him whimper, "Mommy."

CHAPTER 62 - LANCE

Lance's ears ring and rumble. Part of him wonders why ears rumble when you're about to die; then he realizes it's the missile. He still has a mission to complete. He won't fail the way he had. He drags himself across the floor, leaving a dark trail of blood as his head swims and his vision blurs. Lance forces it to focus on the control room door. As he moves his breath comes out in gasps and rasps. Moving closer to his goal, he thinks. *I have to stop it. I have to stop it.* He glances up at a loud mechanical sound to see the gantry and rigging around the missile detach and move away. His mantra changes to *Roxy. Roxy. I love you Roxy.* His strength gives out and Lance collapses, panting. His head and vision swim as he pushes himself up onto his hands then falls flat. He lies on the cold metal floor, unable to move. *I failed. I can't go on. I killed everyone.*

Tears well in Lance's eyes, making his already unfocused vision worse. A small, hard knot forms in his gut. His mind, his being, flee to it, searching for sanctuary. Instead, he envisions Roxy's image, her smile, her pout, her anger, her determination, and the way she looked at him in their moments alone. A surge of energy rushes through him from the point in his gut. The control room door becomes more defined, the colors more vivid. He pushes himself up onto his hands and knees, then scurries forward through the door, only to collapse again as his energy dissipates.

Moaning, he pulls himself up to the control panel and fights to focus on the lights, switches, and display that reads 00:00:30. He stares as the readout counts down to 15, then, realizing what it means, he slams the glowing red button between the keys. A siren blasts three short bursts then goes silent as the button fades to black.

EPILOGUE

The missile, despite its ancient technology, flies straight and true to its target.

The ancient sirens that would have warned the populace had long ago gone silent and decayed. The missile destroys the human population of what used to be known as Boston, all three thousand of them. It also wipes out the scavengers, which outnumber the humans ten to one. The associated firestorm and radiation kills countless more of both for hundreds of miles from the epicenter of the blast and renders uninhabitable large sections of the East Coast. The entire old Northeast corridor is once again devastated. The inhabitants of the surrounding area had not lived through the time of the original blast. Most had heard the old stories passed down parent to child. Those who had survived the original war were changed. So too are the survivors of the Boston blast.

Or it would have—if Viper hadn't stopped it.

Days later, a thousand miles away, a group of humans climbs down the side of a rolling hill. "So when do you think Gov will recall us?" Rudy Arthur asks, biting into a ration wrapper and then spitting it out. He pours the liquid down his throat, crumples the container with one hand, and tosses it aside.

"When he's good and ready," Reggie Edgar, the team leader and gunner, growls back without glancing at his teammate. He continues down the rocky hillside.

Their comms, Roxy Garner, shoots him a glance but says nothing. They all know the sats are down and probably will never come back up. Why was he lying? A flash of light to her right grabs her attention. Her rifle comes up, scope down. Her brim drops down, showing the targets. "Motion, three o'clock. I spot three nasties."

Reggie points up the hill toward the scavengers. "Shock master, take the right." Rudy nods and hustles toward their target. "Telstar, you take the left." Roxy toggles her bud once, acknowledging the command, and moves up the hill. Reggie's rifle comes up and he toggles the bud. "You know what to do. Let's show those nasties what humans can do."

Shock master's voice comes back to SH-1. "Would you look at the size of 'em!"

* * *

ABOUT THE AUTHOR

Serg Koren been writing for longer than he can remember. He writes humorous and somewhat off-beat books. He has written an older children's book, a series of adventures, and a noir, and is currently editing a thriller. Serg writes because he enjoys it, not for the celebrity or money (there is little of that). In his other life, he's an IT expert in fault-tolerant systems (retired), iOS developer, blogger, amateur radio "ham", beer brewer, and foodie. He's also been told he's a cool guy.